THE LAST OUTPOST

Rich Hawkins hails from deep in the West Country, where a childhood of science fiction and horror films set him on the path to writing his own stories. He credits his love of horror and all things weird to his first viewing of John Carpenter's THE THING when, aged twelve, he crept downstairs late one night to watch it on ITV. He has a few short stories in various anthologies, and has written one novella, BLACK STAR, BLACK SUN, released earlier this year. His debut novel THE LAST PLAGUE has recently been nominated for a British Fantasy Award for Best Horror Novel. He currently lives in Salisbury, Wiltshire, with his wife, their daughter and their pet dog Molly. They keep him sane. Mostly.

For my Dad, the bravest person I've ever known.

THE LAST OUTPOST

RICH HAWKINS

Copyright © 2015 Rich Hawkins

This Edition Published 2015 by Crowded
Quarantine Publications
The moral right of the author has been asserted

All characters in this publication are fictitious
and any resemblance to real persons, living or dead,
is purely coincidental.

All rights reserved.
No part of this publication may be reproduced,
stored in a retrieval system, or transmitted, in any
form or by any means without the prior
permission in writing of the publisher, nor be
otherwise circulated in any form of binding or
cover other than that in which it is published
and without a similar condition including this
condition being imposed on the subsequent purchase.

A CIP catalogue record for this book
is available from the British Library

ISBN: 978-0-9932070-9-9

Crowded Quarantine Publications
34 Cheviot Road
Wolverhampton
West Midlands
WV2 2HD

CHAPTER ONE

Royce hid from the monsters beyond the trees in the damp woods. He crouched against a bare grey oak and pulled his rucksack to his chest, his heart lurching at the thrash of dead leaves and snapping sticks. Away to his right, a black and wretched figure flitted between the thin birches. Royce made himself small and close to the ground, squirming and shivering in the cold, a frightened mammal in a hole, his heart squeezed and pulled by muscle and exhaustion. He stifled a sob from gritted teeth as water dripped from strangling branches and screams echoed and slipped through the trees. Animal-like sounds. The lament of the infected. He closed his eyes, counted the rest of his life in chambered heartbeats. If he ran he would be chased, brought down and torn apart.

With the rucksack kept to his chest and his insides like loose stones, he crawled to a shallow trench in the ground and lay on his back amidst the bracken, moss and woodland detritus, staring at the washed out sky until his chest stopped shuddering and the terrified flail of his heart slowed. The dim light faded slowly to darkness. The smell of fungi and dirt in this open coffin of earth. Black beetles crawling over mulch and earthworms burrowing beneath the damp topsoil. A mouse scurried past Royce's face, fleeing the approaching night.

The woods fell silent.

*

It was almost full dark when Royce emerged sweating and wheezing from the trees, pawing at his filthy clothes to remove leaves and thorns. Mist was forming around the low hills under the pale shard of moon. There were no stars and the infected were gone. From where he was standing the horizon opened up and it was all darkness out there. Fields and hedgerows with no one left to tend them. Dormant farmland. The stains of distant towns and villages.

Struggling with the rucksack, he started across the fields. He limped and hurried, casting glances around and over his shoulders, moving in small steps, vulnerable on the open ground. The dark was thickening, like blankets and sheets around him. His torch was in the rucksack, but using it would give away his position to anything stalking the fields. He stumbled over the sodden ground and slippery mud, his old boots worn and tattered. The cold air scraped at his throat as he pulled in each breath, and he kicked his legs and grunted as dull pain shot towards his knees.

Stopping in the middle of the field, he bent over with his hands on his thighs, grimacing at the burning in his chest. He quietened his breathing and listened to the dark around him, attuned to the scurrying of nocturnal creatures. He pulled the collar of his coat around his neck and straightened, then moved on, dismissing a chorus of high-pitched wails as nothing but the wind slipping through winter-bare hedgerows.

The land was haunted, but not by ghosts.

*

The mist caught him as he staggered into the next field. It smelled of damp and mould, and it was all about him like wood smoke. Royce hefted the crowbar in his gloved hands, finding no comfort in its weight. The mud sucked at his boots as he lifted one foot then the other, and patches of the mist dispersed and shrank away as he walked. He halted when he heard awful sounds like an animal being flayed, in the distance. He thought he glimpsed movement at his flanks, and lifted the crowbar to his waist, but there was nothing there.

Across more fields and hawthorn thickets; over ditches of nettles and weeds that wore him down. The temperature was dropping. The night would be close to freezing. He hurried onwards as if lost in a dream, wincing with each step and breathing hard through his dry mouth. He imagined what it would be like to die of exposure, to slowly succumb and fade and then drop to his knees, curl into a shivering form as the cold crept into his limbs and the other parts of him, and then stop his heart while his mind slipped away to happier times and summer gardens of laughter.

He stumbled and slowed, tempted to listen to the voice in the back of his mind that told him to stop, give in, let go, let go of everything that once mattered.

Royce halted when a squat shape of concrete and stone appeared out of the mist. He wiped his eyes with the back of one hand. Glanced over his shoulder then back to the structure, took a hesitant step forwards and swallowed down the rawness in his throat, expecting something to come screaming out of the black doorway.

With the crowbar raised, he suppressed the bile and acid broiling in his chest and approached the structure.

It was a pillbox, built during World War Two, one of the many 'hardened field defences' that once dotted the mainland. Barely taller than Royce, hexagonal-shaped with walls pitted and scarred, dotted with lichen and moss. He stopped before the entrance, where the door had been removed long ago, and took his torch from the rucksack. The cold air dried the sweat on his face. He pulled up the cloth around his neck so that it covered his mouth and nose. Fabric sucked past his lips as he breathed.

Distant sounds out in the mist. Strange calls and keening wails. Cries scraped from wet vocal chords.

He hesitated at the threshold, the mist drifting and sloughing at his back, and he aimed the torch into the dark of the structure's insides. One step. Two steps.

THE LAST OUTPOST

He held his breath and didn't release it until the shadows had retreated from the torchlight. He twisted the crowbar in his grip and considered the force it would take to cave in a human skull.

Then he was past the doorway, and he halted.

Nothing reached for him out of the funhouse dark. Everything dust-caked and old. The smell of shut-in spaces and so many forgotten crypts.

*

The narrow corridor branched into three small bare rooms. No lighting on the dour ceilings. In the event of an invasion, vertical slit-like embrasures in the walls would have been used by infantry as firing holes. The torchlight swam across the ceilings. The floors were furred with dust and crumbled mortar, the interior walls slowly degrading. Rodent droppings and paw prints. Dead insects dried to carapaces and husks. Old stains and spiders' webs with silk cocoons. Something small, feathery and desiccated in one corner.

Royce looked through one embrasure, but then retreated from the opening as if scared the mist would catch his scent and slip into the pillbox to smother him. He played the torch beam around a room. The remains of an old campfire in the middle of the floor. Patches of the walls were blackened. Ash and charcoal crumbled and crunched under his boots, and with his left foot he sifted through the cold ashes and found a scorched photo charred and melted round the edges. A sunny day. Smiles for the camera. A family portrait with the bright blue sea behind them.

He dropped the photo and nudged it back amongst the ashes. By the wall, under the embrasure, were empty tins heaped upon a thick book. He bent, squinting and fretting as he checked the labels. Baked beans, spaghetti hoops, and ravioli. He picked up a tin that once contained peach slices in syrup and inhaled the residual sweetness. His mouth watered; it made him giddy and sad, mournful for lost things. He retrieved the book from underneath the tins and looked at the creased cover. A collection of fairy tales left behind by some nomadic survivor. Royce wondered what became of them.

He shook off the rucksack and settled down in a corner facing the doorway to the corridor. He took out the blanket, the half-eaten packet of cheese crackers and the small bottle of water he was conserving with little sips. His back against the cold wall, he laid the musty blanket over his legs and up to his chest. He gnawed at the crackers and took small mouthfuls of water. The tongue behind his teeth licked the water from the roof of his mouth.

When he found a dust-covered silver penny on the floor by his feet, he cleaned it with his spit and regarded it like the greatest of all things.

*

THE LAST OUTPOST

In the deepening cold he wrapped himself in the stinking blanket and tightened against the wall with his knees drawn to his chest. His teeth chattered as he trembled and watched the doorway and the inky darkness. The smell of ash, his filthy skin and damp clothes.

His eyes closed whenever he let his thoughts wander to brighter days, and his head dropped and nodded as he remembered a warm bed in another life. A mug of hot chocolate and buttered toast. A good book and a takeaway. The memory of prawn crackers brought tears to his eyes.

He smiled a slow, wan smile. Then he thought about his eventual death and that if he fell asleep he might not wake again. And he realised he didn't care too much about that.

CHAPTER TWO

The mist receded in the grey light of dawn. Royce ate a meagre breakfast of half a stale bagel and some peanuts, followed with a few sips of water. Afterwards he scraped his toothbrush over his teeth, then stretched his limbs and winced at the ache in his bones.

He squatted in a dark corner and shat, and when he was finished he wiped his arse with torn away pages of fairy tales.

He left the pillbox as the pale sun climbed the pale sky. It wasn't a safe place to take shelter. He picked his way through other fields, his empty stomach aching and his legs throbbing with dull pain. Yellowed bones scattered over stubbled ground. Curved ribs and slats of vertebrae, pallid jawbones and blunt teeth. A smashed skull and gaping eye sockets, gnawed clean and left in the dirt among the black beetles and patches of pale grass.

Royce took out his binoculars and scanned the broken horizon. A group of deer grazed by a grove of trees, picking at the sparse ground. Crows lifted from the fields and flocked northwards. When he looked again for the deer they were gone. He put away the binoculars and unfolded the tattered map from his back pocket. A red cross marked upon a location. He estimated his position, scratching at his beard, talking nonsense to himself. Not far away now. Maybe a few hours' walk. Maybe more, if he had to stop and rest.

*

He walked alongside a narrow road until it terminated at a T-junction. Two cars, at some point during the outbreak, had suffered a head-on collision. A few yards away, another car was nose-down in a ditch. Further on, a lorry had destroyed a wire fence and was lying on its side like a felled juggernaut in the scarred field.

The wind moved across the road. Royce pulled up his cloth-mask and tightened the straps on the rucksack. He went to the cars on the road and stood looking at the crumpled bonnets, torn bumpers, fractured windscreens and ruined metalwork. Side mirrors hanging on wires. Tyre marks and shattered glass on the tarmac and the grass verges. Scraps of metal and plastic.

Both of the driver's doors were open. He checked one of the cars and found an impact point of dried blood and hair in the cracked windscreen. A pile of bloody bandages on the passenger seat. A man's shoe in the footwell. In the back was a baby seat, which he found himself staring at it until his eyes stung. He went to the other car, a Ford Escort with flat tyres and smashed windows. No bodies. Insurance documents on the seats, all useless and sun-bleached.

And when he walked to the car in the ditch he almost stepped in a bundle of rags and bones and a flap of something leathery that had once been skin.

The car was empty and there was no food to be found.

As the sky grew dark, he entered the field and went to the back of the trailer and put one ear against the door. Held his breath. Silence inside. He unhooked the metal latch and pushed the door so that it opened enough for him to peer inside. He switched on his torch and held it to the dark gap, and he slumped when he ran the light around the empty trailer.

Royce left the door hanging open and walked around to the cab. No way of getting inside unless he climbed up to the passenger door or smashed the windscreen. But when he looked through the mottled glass and saw the driver being absorbed by wet strands of fungus-like flesh, he stepped back and was grateful for the windscreen between them. One side of the driver's face was pressed against the glass, his mouth slack and flowering with writhing blooms. The man's visible eye opened, swollen and livid, and Royce retreated hurriedly towards the road with the sky fading black above him.

*

Royce walked and watched the sky. Thunder crackled in the distance. The wind pulled at him. Willow trees stooped and swayed. Despite his hunger and thirst he bypassed two villages and a small town because he'd heard the warbled shrieks of infected from its desolate streets. The cold gripped him and there was nothing left of the land save the dirt and stone under his boots. He stopped, glanced around then checked the map.

Not far to go. He walked onwards.

*

His heart quickened when he glimpsed a guard tower through a thin line of trees, but he had to stop and rest before he approached the camp. Exhaustion filled him like slow poison. He sat and cast his eyes around. From the rucksack he took a small bag of Maltesers with only three left inside, and popped one between his teeth, savouring the taste on his tongue and the working of his saliva glands before he bit into it. He closed his eyes and thought of home. The silent land around him. A knot in his stomach. No noise from the camp, just the wind prevailing over forgotten fields.

*

He slipped through the trees and emerged into the open. The camp had been raised upon a showground used before the outbreak to stage music festivals, fun fairs and agricultural exhibitions. It was the width of two football pitches alongside each other, surrounded by a tall metal fence and heaped sandbags. Swathes of barbed and razor wire. Empty dens of sandbags where machine gun nests once flanked the entrance. The large gates were hanging open and creaking.

In the field across from the camp, there was a large pile of bodies spilling from a hole. Royce envied the dead in their glistening mounds. From where he stood he could see right through the middle of the camp, where the walkway was muddy between rows of tents and portable cabins.

Through the entranceway, walking slowly until he halted and looked around, the crowbar held at his side, his other hand with its thumb hitched under the strap of the rucksack over his shoulder. Squirm of mud under his boots. Shoeprints and large tyre tracks around him. He was careful not to slip. Silence in the tents and empty spaces. He chewed on his bottom lip and watched the canvas walls of tents flap and billow. The hammer of his heart in his throat. He pulled the hood of his coat over his head as drizzle began to fall.

Turn around and leave. There's nothing here.

He couldn't leave before he'd searched the camp.

It was a village of tents like a third-world slum. Rows of them, all sizes and colours, pinned by metal stakes and anything sharp and sturdy enough to hold them to the earth. Chemical toilets. IBC tanks had been used to store drinking water, but now they were empty and dry.

THE LAST OUTPOST

The ground was waterlogged and muddy, with sparse patches of dead grass. Some tents had collapsed. Paper strewn across the dirt. The taste of ashes in the air and the smell of burnt plastic and wood. People's belongings left behind and children's toys scattered on the ground. A metal bucket filled with sand and cigarette ends. Lawn furniture, tables and chairs. Sodden, stained blankets. Dresses and jackets on clothes hangers idled on the side of tents and washing lines. A bicycle with a buckled wheel. Bins full of rubbish and rotting food. Stacked wooden pallets and mounds of trash. A plastic bag was stuffed with twenty pound notes. The cold ashes of abandoned campfires and the skittering of rats through the cold walkways.

The signs of a hurried abandonment. A forced evacuation. But to where? Tears pricked his eyes and a cold knot formed in his stomach. He imagined the terrified refugees led from this place by soldiers and taken back out into the ruins of the country. Trying to escape the mainland, Royce assumed. He had heard the stories. He had heard what happened at Sidmouth.

Past washing lines heavy with hanging clothes, he stared at a line of occupied body bags. Scattered marbles in the grass. Dirt and puddles. A biohazard suit left on the ground like the sloughed skin of some alien creature. The entrances to tents were hungry mouths.

The only body he found was a man who seemed to have set himself on fire. A foetal shape shrivelled and blackened, with gritted teeth too white. An empty can of petrol and a lighter lying in the scorched grass not far from where his corpse had fallen. He smelled like wet charcoal and barbecued pork. Royce walked away when his mouth began to water.

The field hospital at the heart of the camp had been ransacked. Rows of empty beds, some of them overturned. Nothing left to salvage, it seemed. No bodies. Smashed equipment and dirty bandages. A bin filled with used syringes and medical instruments coated in dried blood. Royce searched through drawers and storage boxes, and all he found was a box of waterproof plasters and some anti-bacterial wipes. Nothing else.

In one tent, where the blankets upon a bed were damp, lumpy and stinking, he found a holdall filled with jars of baby food. Some of the small jars were smashed or cracked, but a dozen or so were intact and sealed, so he pocketed them and thought himself lucky.

He searched the mess tent, walking among the tables dotted with plates of rotting food. He picked up a steel ladle encrusted with mouldy porridge, looked at it with dull curiosity, then placed it back in the cooking pot where he'd found it.

Moments later he was crouched trembling in one of the walkways with his hands balled into fists and pressed against his mouth. When he held his hands before his face, they were shaking as if with palsy. His heart felt too large and too fast, fed by the terror of being alone for the rest of his life. Left behind.

He wandered among the camp as the light waned and shadows filled empty spaces. A dog howled in the distance and it was the most mournful sound he had heard in living memory.

*

Royce heard the mewling above the dry rattle of the wind, and he walked towards the sound, and it grew louder until he was almost upon it. He stopped before a ramshackle tent still wet from the last downpour. A canvas flap shifted in the breeze and lifted to reveal oily darkness and the suggestion of movement.

The mewling stopped.

Using the crowbar he slowly lifted the flap and peered in. The sudden daylight, even as grey as it was, showed him the inside of the tent. He stepped back but remained in the entranceway, his stomach turning to soup.

A woman and her baby lying on a camp bed.

"Oh my god," Royce whispered.

The baby was sucking upon the woman's breast, its mouth melded to her skin. Most of the baby's body was attached to the woman, as if the infant were some kind of parasite. The baby was a gaunt and squirming thing with a bloated stomach, knotted with tumours and cysts. Its tiny hands looked normal. A head of wispy hair. It would have only been several months old when it was infected along with its mother. Maybe it had been born just before the outbreak started.

The mother began to coo to the baby. Crimson veins down the woman's face and neck. The shadow of her pale scalp underneath her thinning hair. Her mouth was sharp and sore, and a glistening tongue lurked beyond her scabbed lips. One side of her skirt was hitched up, exposing one thin leg and a dirty knee. Her vest was shorn of one strap, and her left breast was hanging down, veiny and engorged, sustenance for the feeding baby.

Royce was silent. The day fading behind him. Bursts of thunder far away. He lowered the crowbar as his face became slack and cold, because there was no threat from the woman, just the echoes of the person she used to be before the world ended. He stepped away and let the canvas flap drop. Staring at the tent, he didn't move for a long time, his hands worrying at each other until he found the conviction to finally move and leave this dead place.

The camp would be there for years, battered by rain and snow, hailstones and storms, until it was finally consumed by the land.

CHAPTER THREE

Stumbling down tumbledown tracks and bridleways, past burnt-down farms as he dragged his rucksack behind him and glimpsed the bones of livestock in the black ruins. He looked at the sky and let the rain dampen his face. His feet pained him. At the roadside he sheltered in an abandoned car whose windscreen was plastered with brown leaves and detritus. Smell of leather upholstery and the old world. No keys. Cigarette ends in the ashtray, and an empty Starbucks cup in the drinks holder. A book of baby names with certain pages folded at the corners. *C for Catherine. M for Michael.* In the glove compartment was a packet of mints, and he ate them one at a time with the downpour upon the car as he mourned for the infected, for the dead, and for the world lost to the plague.

*

After the rain stopped, Royce left the car and walked on, aimless and lost with the scuttle of dead leaves around him. He skirted a village where the cries of abominations echoed through barren streets and gardens. A mile later he stopped in the road when he saw a house ahead and set back from the right side of the road at the end of a long driveway.

Losing the light in the sky, or what light there was on days like those, as the grey afternoon sloughed into darkness. He needed to find shelter for the night, and his legs couldn't carry him much further. Blisters burned on his feet and made him wince with each step. Callouses and bruises. Cold and aching, a patchwork man made by clumsy hands.

Past thin trees and telephone poles with sagging wires, Royce clambered over a muddy bank and cut across a waterlogged field to the rear of the house. The sky was the colour of dull steel. A magpie watched him from the shelter of a dripping bough. There was thunder far behind him, chasing his heels. He hobbled across stones and dirt and mud, slowing until he had almost stopped. A thin wooden fence protected the back garden, and he rested behind it and listened. He was just tall enough to peer over the fence and glimpse the back of the property. A lawn that hadn't been mown in months or longer. A fishpond. A child's trampoline. The curtains drawn in the windows. The back door was shut. Royce grabbed the rim of the fence and pulled himself up, hoping it wouldn't collapse under his weight. Splinters dug into his gloves. The fence trembled as he swung one leg over the rim, followed by the rest of his shivering form, and he tumbled to the grass on the other side and landed on an ankle, which turned awkwardly. He collapsed on to his back and cried out.

THE LAST OUTPOST

He put his hands to his ankle, sat against the fence and waited for the pain to fade. Sweat beaded his face and dampened his thick beard. It was just a light sprain. He sighed and wiped his face. When he put out his hands and stood, biting his lip, the ankle held, but hurt when he moved it. A break would have been the end of him.

He began limping towards the back of the house. A plastic heron staked at the edge of the fishpond. Small rocks and garden ornaments. The water was stagnant, like oil. The remains of a goldfish floating on the surface. Flaps of orange-gold skin and the nub of a tiny spine. Most of the meat eaten away. Other goldfish lurked below the surface, flashes of colour in the murk. The runt of the group had been set upon and devoured.

At the end of the lawn were two makeshift graves. The bare earth had been flattened, and at the head of each grave a crude cross had been fashioned from sticks entwined with string. The graves were deep enough to discourage scavengers. Royce remembered digging a grave not so long ago, while sirens wailed and streets were full of slaughter and fire. A grave for two bodies, so they'd be together in the earth. The sheer effort it took to carve a hole out of the dirt. The act of wrapping loved ones in blanket-shrouds and lowering them into the ground. Covering them with soil to honour the old traditions.

His ankle flared with pain and he leaned against the outer wall with deep breaths shuddering in his chest. The windows were clouded with grime. He tried the door and pushed; it didn't give, but after a while of prying the jamb with the crowbar, the door pulled away from him with a low crack and swung inwards into the dark. He paused on the threshold, muttering to himself, his arms throbbing from the effort of busting the locked door. Paranoid about booby-traps, he looked for silk-thin trip-wires attached to shotguns triggers or slicing blades. He'd had nightmares about breaking into a house and sticking his foot into razor-toothed steel jaws. He worried about severed arteries and amputated legs, and catching tetanus from rusting metal. He worried about bleeding out and dying alone because there were more mundane, albeit just as lethal, infections to be caught if care wasn't taken.

The house was dark before him.

*

The low howl of the wind under the eaves. Dust in the stale air. The sigh of shifting walls painted with oil-slick shadows as Royce steered the torchlight around the kitchen. He pulled back the curtains and closed the back door, then slanted a wooden chair under the handle to keep it shut. Dead electrical appliances like obscure relics. Crumbs and mould on the worktops. Fridge magnets from animal parks. A circular dining table with a newspaper and some magazines piled next to salt and pepper shakers and a bowl of hardened sugar. The dirty linoleum floor squealed under the slip of his boots as he tried the lights and other switches, but everything was dead. Through an open doorway, a hallway ran to the front of the house.

Royce stood and listened, glancing at framed photos on the Welsh dresser of a middle-aged couple with a girl in her early teens. Happier times. Their smiles made him feel sick and lonely. In the mausoleum silence he stared at the photos until his eyes stung and he looked away. He was tempted to check the cupboards for food, but his priority was to clear the house and ensure he was alone.

Into the hallway, soft steps and the muffled rhythm of his breathing. Compressing lungs and a trembling heart as the torchlight speared the darkness. The air tasted old and sour. Coats on a rack were slouching shapes reaching for the floor, but nothing hungry lurked in the shadows. He hoped if any infected were upstairs they would have heard him and come down by now. But not all infected were so obvious in their hunting methods.

He picked up a cordless telephone from its cradle and put it to his ear just to remember a simple act from another life. All those things taken for granted. He closed his eyes to the silence, trying to imagine a human voice at the other end of the line, a voice saying his name. Cold callers or loved ones. Anyone. It seemed ridiculous now, for voices to have been connected over such distances.

He looked at the ceiling and its fine fractures, and remembered the horrors he'd found in other houses and buildings he'd searched in the days following the spread of the plague. Nests and dens in blocks of flats. The lairs of monsters in bungalows and council houses. Silent tombs and charnel houses. In a house just outside Taunton he'd found the rooms turned into larders for creatures that liked to ripen their meat before consuming it. Naked bodies hanging from resin-like secretions on the walls. A man squirming for breath inside a glistening cocoon.

Royce was adamant he would never end up like that, trussed up and helpless, food for obscene appetites.

He opened both sets of curtains in the living room, which looked out into both the front and back gardens. He watched dust rise and fall and settle upon the dulled furniture. Watery daylight killed his shadow. Dead flowers in vases on the windowsills, their petals like flakes of slowly crumbling ash. The driveway was empty, as was the road beyond.

Oil paintings on the walls. Beige wallpaper, domestic and dour. Empty boxes of Ritz crackers. Old newspapers scattered around the room. Royce noticed headlines from the days before the outbreak – a celebrity divorce, lying politicians, trouble in the Middle East and religious fundamentalists protesting against gay marriage. On the coffee table were empty cans of Lilt, Tango and Pepsi, and encrusted cutlery upon dirty plates. Plastic folders stacked into fragile towers. A bookcase crammed with old and creased paperbacks. A glass cabinet full of someone else's memories and mementoes. Porcelain ornaments on the mantelpiece above the fireplace blocked with piled stones and bricks: a defensive measure against the infected, because some monsters were not averse to scuttling down chimneys to reach their prey.

Candles had burned down to dregs of oily wax and charred wicks. He picked up a box of matches then dropped it when he shook it and nothing rattled inside. Amidst the relics and the grey light Royce saw the reflection of himself in the television. He was a wraith, a shade, a figment made of straw and feathers. Something barely real. He picked through the mess and nudged an empty water bottle with one foot. No more recycling, ever again, and all of it like dusty relics.

*

The stairway creaked under his weight as he climbed towards darkness. The torchlight was a spear. His nerve endings tingled and he swallowed a lump in his throat. He opened the curtains in the small window on the landing and paused to check his grip of his hand around the crowbar. Four closed doors to four shut away rooms. Did he want to see what waited inside them? The shift of his feet answered and he opened the door to the bathroom, where he found drops of dried blood in the bath. He turned the taps and there was only the dry rattle of pipes in the walls. No water in the toilet. When he saw what remained of himself in the mirror above the sink he turned away quickly. The push of his bones against his face. To see his grinning skull leering back at him like something excavated from a pile of steaming rags.

Then he was standing in the girl's bedroom between the pink and white walls. Cuddly toys cradling their hearts. Posters of pop bands and cartoon characters, photos in heart-shaped frames, and a dressing table with a jewellery box, hairbrushes and a notebook with CASSIE'S DIARY – KEEP OUT written on the front cover, secured with a tiny padlock of shiny metal.

In the master bedroom he found an empty bed and strewn sheets, a wardrobe filled with old-smelling clothes that reminded him of Oxfam shops. Nothing of any use to him.

When he opened the door to the last room he had to step back from the smell of dry decay. The woman was hanging from the ceiling by a rope slung over a wooden beam. He went into the room. The skin shrivelled tight on her sunken face, mummified like a desert-corpse. Dull teeth glimpsed through her frozen mouth, curtained by straw-like hair. Her wide-open eyes never left Royce, and he stepped back from the rot-stink and the dried-out lumps of her body within the dressing gown holding her together. A spider crawled across one bare leg and vanished into the swaddled folds.

THE LAST OUTPOST

Royce lowered his head towards the floor and mourned her, for she had been beautiful.

CHAPTER FOUR

He cut the woman down and wrapped her in a blanket then laid her in a corner of the room. When he checked the attic for nasty surprises he found last year's Christmas decorations and a colony of mice scurrying about the dust and forgotten things.

As the light faded in the early dusk and the wind shrieked like graveside mourners, he secured the house and closed the curtains, then lit a candle against the dark.

*

The kitchen cupboards were bare except for a small bag of salted peanuts and a tin of green beans. He turned the tin over in his hands and inspected it for punctures, grimacing in the candlelight. It was sealed tight and intact. When he opened the fridge he shrank away from the cloying, choking stench of rotting ham and eggs. Its interior was alive with mould and crawling insects.

He picked through the rooms, checking the hideaway places, his shadow becoming something spindly from the flickering flame he carried. Afterwards, he sat in the living room and went through the useful things he'd scavenged. A bottle of apple schnapps pulled from the back of a cupboard in the utility room out the back. The green beans and the peanuts. A meal fit for pilgrims and drifters.

He had found the girl's stash of chocolate under her bed: over a dozen bars of chocolate and a small box of Quality Street. The unexpected find did little to lift the darkness from his mind, and only served to remind him of Christmas afternoons in front of the television.

Next to the stash had been a laptop in a travel case. He sat back on the sofa and set the laptop down on his thighs. In the half-light it seemed like a piece of fantastical machinery from another age. He remembered Wi-Fi and broadband and search engines. He missed social media. What had his last Facebook status been? His final tweet? It had all been so fragile. A world of small concerns and problems.

He switched the laptop on and waited while it powered up, aware of how fast his heart kicked. The glow from the monitor hurt his eyes but made him smile. The battery was fully-charged. Files and icons on a desktop background of snowy mountains in some glacial landscape. Somewhere beautiful and far away. Royce took a few minutes to acquaint himself with the keyboard and the mouse pad. His fingers moved hesitantly. Unsurprisingly the internet was down. He snorted. No more Google. And he went through the files, aware that there were only a few hours left in the battery. There were documents; photos of holidays in France and Spain. White beaches and Disney-blue skies he'd never seen in real life.

The media player was full of music by saccharine pop bands, so he opened another file, which listed a number of romantic films, musicals and Pixar cartoons.

He watched *WALL-E* while he gorged on the Quality Street and schnapps, and found himself crying at the end of the film. The alcohol swam in his blood and numbed his face, flushed his skin with warmth. His vision blurred as he drank. He finished the box of chocolates and moaned while he held his cramping stomach.

The laptop died halfway through *Moulin Rouge*, so he sat in the dim light of the candle and stared at the monitor and drank the schnapps. From his rucksack he took out a small plaster cast with a little handprint forged into it. He touched the delicate shapes of tiny fingers and a thumb, a memory of a smiling baby girl so small and perfect and fragile, and the pressure behind his eyes was too much and he put his face in his hands and cried.

He fell into a sleep where he dreamed of empty cities in an empty world, and all the people he once knew were either dead or missing or lost to the plague when Britain fell. Later, he woke in a feverish stupor and imagined the dead woman upstairs slowly coming to life, unfolding her awful form from the blanket then padding down the stairs to welcome him into her home. Then he slept again.

THE LAST OUTPOST

*

Royce was woken by a thumping beyond the walls. He sat up, rubbing his eyes and groaning. His mouth tasted of sour apples and bile. An unknown amount of time had passed, and he felt used up and worn down, a shape made of bruised flesh and sinew. His ears rang and his head pulsed in time with his heartbeat. He thought he had dreamt the thumping until he heard it upon the front door. It sounded frantic and panicked. He rose and wilted, held out his arms for balance with a blanket around him, then winced as a sharp pain flared in his ankle. He leaned against the wall and gritted his teeth until it passed.

A man's voice, cracking with fear, called out as Royce hobbled into the dark of the narrow hallway and stood back from the door. The man was pleading to be let inside and hammering on the door so hard it rattled on its hinges. Royce stood back and stared at the door. He swallowed hard down his throat and into his gullet. His stomach was all knotted and gurgling. He breathed through the holes in his face.

"Let me in! Please let me in!"

The man's cries were getting louder and more desperate, but Royce didn't move, because his legs felt concrete-set and he couldn't lift his feet from the floor. He wished that the man would leave the door alone, and his hands curled and uncurled at his sides as he backed against the wall.

"Let me in!"

It could be a trick, Royce thought. Could be a ruse to lure him out and open the doors, so the man could take the house for himself. Maybe there were others out there, watching from a distance, waiting and planning. Thieves and murderers. Maybe they had been watching the house since he'd arrived.

The man went to each downstairs window in turn, fumbling and banging on the glass. He wouldn't be able to smash through the double-glazing unless he had something heavy duty, or a gun. Then Royce heard the back door being tried, and he held his breath, but the barricade held. The man circled back to the front of the house and shouted again. Royce crouched against the wall in the dark and folded his arms over his chest and laid them on his knees. He rocked back and forth as the man shouted, swore and threw himself at the door.

An inhuman scream came from the beyond the house. The man began sobbing, and Royce wanted to let him in, but he didn't move from the wall even though he was ashamed of his cowardice and hated himself for it.

*

Royce limped up the stairway to the window on the landing, where he pulled back a flap of curtain and looked outside. The man was stumbling across the adjacent field away from the house and the road, tripping and flailing, a rucksack hanging from one shoulder and slowing him down. Even from fifty yards away the emaciation of the man's body was obvious through his ragged clothing. He was no member of a murderous gang; he was just another desperate survivor, no different than Royce.

A pack of infected emerged from a dark thicket into the field. There were seven of them, awful shapes in the pale light; ravenous and wasted. Limbs twisted with horrid movements and mouths snapping at the air. They sighted the man across the field and set after him. The man looked back once, then stumbled and tripped, falling to his knees as the rucksack fell from his shoulder. He rose and staggered onwards, then realised he'd left the rucksack behind, but when he turned around the infected were within forty yards of him and he slumped as he seemed to accept he couldn't reach the bag before the infected reached him. So he stumbled onwards, but he didn't make it far before he stopped again. He was crying, his head lowered, his hands making a gesture of prayer.

It all happened very quickly.

The infected fell upon him and he was lost beneath the writhing bodies and grabbing hands, and all those mouths.

The man was dismantled and emptied upon the field and his opened body steamed into the cold air.

CHAPTER FIVE

Royce lay on the sofa with a photo of his family in one hand. He was a lumpen shape under the blankets. The guilt inside him like the weight of stones. Acid broiled in his stomach and made him nauseous. Maybe he had done the right thing, because if he'd let the man into the house, the infected would have followed.

It gave him no comfort.

He mouthed the names of his wife and his daughter and mourned them through the dark hours as the infected wailed in the desolate fields.

He did not sleep that night.

*

The dawn came like the rise of something unclean beyond the curve of the Earth. Birdsong woke him, and he went to a window and peered outside to see that the infected were gone. His ankle felt better, although he was careful when he moved and each step was taken slowly through the cold house. He dry-heaved into the toilet then leaned against the bowl and closed his eyes. He stayed that way for a while, but then his legs began to stiffen, so he stood and went downstairs.

THE LAST OUTPOST

*

His breakfast was a Mars bar and some water. The craving for a strong, sweet coffee and buttered toast with sliced banana darkened his mood. He gathered his remaining supplies and left the house. The morning was dull and cold. He wondered how long it was till Christmas or if it had already passed.

He went down to where the infected had killed the man, and scattered the crows who'd been feeding on the scraps. They settled upon a nearby tree and watched him, waiting for him to leave. He stood over the remains, whispering an apology. He asked for forgiveness, but the wind that slipped past him and over the fields was indifferent to the suffering of men.

There wasn't much left of the man, and what there was stained the damp grass, all gristle and splintered bones, hair and sinew. Pale white skin. The leftover bits of him. His clothes had been torn into wet scraps. There was a wedding ring among the remains. A boot with a foot inside it, severed at the ankle.

Drag marks and footprints on the ground. The smell of exposed innards and raw meat. He remembered when he was a boy and his mother used to bring bones home from the butcher's shop for the dogs. The popping sounds of the bones as the dogs chewed at them. He pictured slavering wet mouths, but not those of his old pets.

Royce left what remained of the man on the grass for the scavengers and walked over to the rucksack. It was untouched. He watched it for a while, as if he were afraid something squirming and damp would erupt from it. Then he crouched and opened the rucksack. He glanced over his shoulders then looked inside, reached in and pulled out a notebook. He turned it over in his hand then leafed through the pages. It was a plague journal. A photo of a boy in a school uniform fell out and landed by Royce's feet. He picked it up and looked at it, then placed it on top of the journal and laid them on the ground. He also found an old James Herbert paperback, a Darth Vader action figure, and a matchbox containing a few clippings of auburn hair. Half a roll of toilet paper and a bottle of silted water. At the bottom of the rucksack was a leather wallet with fifty pounds in ten pound notes, two credit cards, a driver's license, a blood donor card, and a receipt from an Esso petrol station in Yeovil. Royce checked the driver's license and read the man's name, as if doing so would honour him in death.

"Ben Ottway," Royce whispered. The words were taken by the cold air. "I should have helped you, Ben."

He pocketed the toilet paper then replaced the photo of the boy inside the journal and returned it to the rucksack along with the other items he didn't need.

THE LAST OUTPOST

Royce shouldered his rucksack and moved on, his boots pressing into the sodden ground. He turned back once to the house and it was as dark and silent as when he first arrived.

*

He was directionless and lost, and the land accepted him for the shambling wreck he had become. Aimless in the dimming light, he considered turning around and heading back to the house, but it was easier to keep his feet shuffling down the road. If he had stayed at the house, the infected would have found him eventually, and he would have ended up like the man he'd refused to help.

Distant thunder in the west, trying to catch him. He stopped in the road and poked the toe of his boot at a vague pile of human skin; it had been sloughed, like snakeskin. Moulted. Leading away from the skin and into the scrub at the side of the road was a trail of drying slime. He didn't follow the trail. No good would come of it.

He walked onwards, watching a thin plume of smoke on the northern horizon. A burning house, perhaps. Didn't matter. He was inured to it all, the destruction of what used to be.

He saw a buzzard feeding on the corpse of an infected man by the roadside. Rending the flesh with hooked talons. The bird raised its reddened beak at Royce until he passed. He thought about the possibility of the plague jumping species. At least if the plague was contained just to humans, the other animal species would stand a chance of survival. If it did manage to jump from humans to other animals, that could mean the destruction of all life on the planet.

*

Later.

Glancing over his shoulder, back at the road behind him, because he was sure he was being followed. He walked for what felt like hours, exhausted and thirsty, drying out and weakening with each step. He stopped in the middle of the road and looked at the cats' eyes glinting like cheap pound shop jewellery. Tears on his face. A pressure behind his sternum and a scratch in his throat that wouldn't go away. He shrugged off the rucksack and drank from the water bottle until he was coaxing the last drops into his mouth. Then he returned the bottle to its place and bent over with his hands on his thighs. His face was hot and clammy, sweat leaking from the pores. Dry mouth. He had expected this, sooner or later, sleeping rough and living in squalor. A hole in his stomach he couldn't fill. His vision dimmed and the road crawled under his feet. He rubbed his knuckles against his eyes and when he took them away there were nonsense afterglow shapes in all he could see. His cough was deep, hacking and wet. There was mucus in his phlegm when he spat.

He raised his head and looked far down the road. His wife was standing there, out of focus and dulled like an old photograph. A frail image in danger of being swept away by the wind. She was smoke and ash, beauty and darkness.

Royce didn't believe in ghosts, not even in this world.

She's not a phantom, but she's not real. You know that.

But he wanted some comfort, something to soften reality's razor edges. Anything to keep the darkness away for a while. It was exhausting to be scared all of the time.

He straightened and shouldered the rucksack, and walked towards her. He would have smiled, but he'd lost the muscle memory of such a simple act. As he went to her, he was faintly aware of the approaching thunder and the skies ready to open, and he was almost upon her when she held her arms open for him. And in the second it took Royce to see it wasn't his wife, the woman lunged towards him all ruined and wheezing, a thin shape in clotted rags. He saw her eyes. Her nose. Her face.

Her pretty mouth with all its dreadful teeth.

CHAPTER SIX

Royce sagged on the grass verge by the roadside and watched the woman's corpse twitch on the tarmac. The crowbar was by his feet, matted and bloodied with pulped meat, scraps of bone and hair. He whimpered when he saw the blood on his gloves and he took them off and dropped them to the grass. The light was fading and the wind screamed over the low rises and slopes. His entire body was trembling and bile pressed hotly at the back of his throat. He spat until the sour taste left his mouth. A flash of lightning from the direction he'd come. The approaching storm. Deep concussion of thunder. The woman finally went still. Her body was infested with tumours and lesions. Her face was gone and a pale tubular appendage hung limply from what remained of her mouth.

Royce shivered. Cold running through him. It took so much effort to take a life.

*

Almost full dark. He shrank away from the roaring sky and walked through the rain to wash the blood from his clothes. He needed to be cleansed.

THE LAST OUTPOST

An overturned car offered no shelter among the shapes of twisted bodies inside and dark stains on the fractured windows. No shelter on the road, and he thought he would die of exposure out in the darkness.

Lightning exposed the landscape in half-second glimpses. There were dozens of figures in the fields, motionless and staring at the sky. His heart froze and he stopped and looked up to where the lightning revealed a gigantic dark shape in the clouds. Something immense he'd seen during the first days of the outbreak. The rain stung his face and took his breath. And as he stared at the shape it seemed to drill pressure into his eyes, and he turned away clutching his face.

There was woodland ahead and to the right, running alongside the road from across a field. Black trees backlit by bursts of brilliant white light. A sanctuary from the storm. He would deal with whatever waited amongst the trees.

He made for the woods, struggling against the driving rain, dragging his crumpled body past the charred ruins of abandoned vehicles. Through the trees under the dripping canopy, Royce stumbled and fell like a blind beggar. Stray, low limbs scratched his face and snagged on his clothes, and he held his hands in front of his eyes to protect them as he staggered through bracken and undergrowth, leaves and sticks and dead branches. Thunder echoed and chased him through the narrow gaps between the trees.

The sensation of being circled and that circle being tightened to meet him. He shook it off and kept moving, cringing at the touch of branches like so many reaching fingers. He tripped on hard roots bulging from the ground and he fell onto his stomach and the air was knocked out of him. He gasped and spat. Groaned in his throat. Hot needles in his bad ankle. The rain fell onto the trees. He rose and limped onwards, slumping against the dark trunks and their shadows, until he emerged into a small clearing where the ground was waterlogged and his feet splashed through cold puddles. He stopped and caught his breath, his chest heaving and tight, the woods dripping around him. A dark muddled shape ahead of him in the middle of the clearing. Rain upon canvas and plastic. He fumbled for his torch and kept the light low to the ground. The knife he had taken from the last house was clenched in his fist.

A half-collapsed one-man tent, torn and slashed but still intact. Sagging with dead leaves and grime. Barely standing in the hard rain. He directed the torch at the opening in the tent, and nothing moved in there or emerged to meet him. With the knife held out he crouched, then crawled into the tent and swung the torch around. A dry floor. No bodies or signs of violence. No blood. Nothing but empty soft drinks cans and food wrapping. He lay down in the cramped shelter like an animal that had found a place to die. He pulled the zip down, closing the entrance, and took the rucksack from his back and hugged it to his chest as he curled into a squalid mound, clutching the knife in one hand as the storm raged and crashed, and rain lashed the tent. The creak and rattle of trees in the wind. His teeth were chattering. Even his bones were cold.

Royce closed his eyes, soaked and shivering, frightened in the dark of the woods.

*

In dreams, his neighbours hunted him through the back gardens and narrow roads of his hometown. His pet dog eviscerated on the front lawn. A burning house in the distance.

A dream, but also a memory.

When he woke the storm had moved on and dawn had arrived and gone. He was still clutching his rucksack, unmoved from the night before. His clothes were still damp and now he stank like something dragged from a marsh. His bones ached and he gasped for water. A damp heat behind his sternum. Wheezing with every breath scraped from his heavy, sodden lungs. He coughed into his chest and groaned as the inside of the tent swayed and crawled.

He raised his head to the sounds outside the tent. Something working at the ground with a snout and paws, snuffling through the dirt. He moved the knife away from his body and pulled the zipper down a little and peered from the hole. Even the grey light hurt his eyes, and he blinked, lowered his face from the sky and the black trees. The snuffling became a low growl, joined by another. Two white poodles stared at Royce in his shelter, their teeth bared, and he stared back at them, stifling a cough in his throat.

The poodles were half-starved, mangy creatures, and they slowly backed away from Royce as he pulled down the zipper and slouched on his knees in the mouth of the tent. He looked into their wild eyes. Fur coated with grime. They whimpered and growled until they turned and bolted into the trees.

Royce pulled out the map and studied it on his lap. He had a vague idea of his location. He sat there for a while and forced himself to eat a chocolate bar. Movement was a struggle, and he swayed when he climbed to his feet. Aching and weary. Hot skin dripping sweat. He spat and muttered as the wind swept through the tops of the trees. Birds called in the early light.

He pulled on the rucksack and left the clearing behind.

*

Struggling through the woods, his arms around his chest, the knife stored up one sleeve like a magic trick. Easy to imagine ghosts out in the trees and spend forever searching for them. He clutched at his chest and retched into troughs of dead leaves and weeds. His eyes watered and the trees swam in and out of focus. Stinking mulch under his feet. Animal sounds in the distance. If he collapsed, he wouldn't get up again.

The trees all around him. He caught movement at his flanks. Mammals of the woods and birds in the trees. The cold found his skin. He licked moisture from gnarled oaks and birches.

Further on he encountered a white stag feeding from the sodden ground. Royce halted, open-mouthed, careful to keep his distance. In awe of the magnificent thing. The stag turned its head and looked at him. The temptation to reach out and try to touch the animal, to make sure it was real and not some fever-illusion.

"I'm surprised you're still alive," Royce whispered, his voice like nails over sandpaper. "I thought the infected would have caught you by now."

The stag was not afraid of him.

Royce slouched against the nearest tree. "I guess you could say the same to me, mate." He coughed hard and hunched over with spit on his lips, and when he raised his face again the white stag was gone and Royce was alone again.

"Good luck out there," he said and walked onwards.

*

He reached the edge of the woods soon after, and emerged into a dank meadow where the grass smelled of brine and soaked his jeans up to his knees.

Slowworms and adders hid from his clumsy footsteps. He stopped and looked beyond the meadow and the fields beyond it. In the distance, the dark shape of a village. Sloped roofs and squat chimneys. A slash of grey road. No sign of life.

A piercing cry on the low breeze startled him.

Royce walked further into the long grass, dragging his rucksack behind him.

CHAPTER SEVEN

Under the sky of grey he stumbled onto the road and rested to cough up the thick phlegm from his throat. Crows circled overhead, waiting for him to fall. He entered the village from the south.

The doors had been ripped away from a Ford Focus skewed across the middle of the road, and its windscreen was smashed to pale shards. Another car had stopped not far behind. Royce grimaced at the small, ravaged skeleton curled up on the backseat. Little shoes. Leathery sinew. All dried up and broken.

A fire had consumed a row of terraced houses on one side of the road. He picked through the remains but there was nothing he could use. He stepped on a jawbone among the charred wood and ash. Lawns blackened, the grass scorched away. Flowerbeds nothing more than burnt patches of earth. A bird table leaning to one side, stained with soot.

Some doors were open, shadows beyond each threshold. The windows were dark. A motorbike had veered from the road, smashed through a wooden fence and into an ornamental rock pool. The rider was gone.

There were bones in the gardens. Scatterings of carrion. Everything silent and still, a photo into which he had intruded. He cast his eyes around then leaned on a low stone wall at the foot of a garden and coughed until his lungs burned and his chest ached with needling pain. Wiped his streaming eyes and tried not to imagine the infected unfurling themselves from their dens and hiding places and coming out into the street to embrace him. He sighed, closed his eyes against his swaying vision. There had to be a shop somewhere on the main road through the village. If not, he'd have to go house-to-house and hope to find something in those silent rooms full of fading memories and forgotten shades.

He rested behind the cover of a wrecked car and waited for the tightness in his chest to fade. His slumping heart, grey and tired. In the driver's seat of the car, a body stripped to yellowed bone leered at the cracked windscreen covered in dust and dead leaves. Royce peered around the side of the car at the lifeless street ahead. Distant calls of the infected as they stalked the low hills. And the cry of a large bird somewhere out there, maybe a buzzard or a hawk. The rustle of litter drifting against kerbs or into gutters. Kicked by his feet. The smell of old death in the air, ingrained like a chemical taint. He supposed all the villages were like this now – cold, barren and tainted.

Royce moved down the street, boots scraping on the road. Crunch of grit underneath him. Every step taken slow and careful. He watched the windows above and around him.

THE LAST OUTPOST

Ahead, crows and magpies pecked at ripped rubbish bags, squabbling over rotting scraps and chicken bones. The magpies bullied the crows, outnumbering them. The crows flapped away as Royce approached, but the magpies didn't move and regarded him with sullen, black eyes.

A car had crashed into a streetlight. A human femur wedged in a storm drain. He walked over envelopes littering the street. Ahead was a Royal Mail delivery van with its back doors open, and its contents of parcels and envelopes had spilled out onto the road, rain-sodden and thin, like stains in the tarmac; some of the envelopes flitted around the street, picked up by the wind and caught by bushes and the low branches of trees, scattered upon overgrown lawns.

Royce's heart flinched as he saw movement far ahead on the straight, stretching road littered with abandoned cars. A glimpse of a piece of clothing. A flash of colour. His stomach turned to glass when he saw the swarm of infected emerge from around the corner. He stared at them for perhaps too long, then snapped out of his dull, dry-mouthed shock and climbed into the back of the Royal Mail van. He moved slowly, carefully, and pulled his rucksack alongside him among the mounds of envelopes and crumpled parcels. He winced at the noise the doors made as he pulled them shut, and was shocked by the complete darkness that swallowed him. He sat still, breathing hard, as the sounds of wet mouths, bestial grunts and slapping feet grew closer until they were louder than the frantic kicking of his heart. The van trembled around him. The sounds of a thousand beating drums. Screams and howls from hungry hearts. He buried his face in his hands and bowed his head as the swarm passed around the van. Knockings and scrapings on the sides of the vehicle. Wedding rings, bracelets, watches and jagged nails. Wet slopping of tendrils. Skittering of busy feet. Deafening, awful sounds. Something wheezed against the back of the van and Royce kept his head lowered and his eyes closed because he didn't want to see the terrible face of the thing that would rip the doors open and pull him from his shelter.

He clasped his hands to his ears and whimpered lowly under his breath. His bladder slackened. He dared not loosen a cough from his throat. He thought of happier days and the sun of an English summer on his face. His mother's voice calling him home for dinner. When he was a little boy, playing football with his father in the back garden. His wife in a hospital bed, screaming and crying and pushing as he held her hand and whispered that he loved her and she was the bravest woman he'd ever met. And then a new life wailing from new lungs. He cut the umbilical cord with shaking hands. His daughter handed to him, a grey little thing wrapped in blankets and topped with a little woollen hat. She looked up at him with the large curious eyes of a newborn. The wonder of the world she'd been born into. The love and the pain and all she would experience. The swell of Royce's heart. His wife smiling at him, tears in her eyes, pale and exhausted.

And then they were taken from him when he opened his eyes. The swarm moved away. His shivering heart was all he could hear in the lonely dark. The silent aftermath of the infected's passage. The creak of the van's suspension in a sudden gust of howling wind.

He didn't move for a long time, too scared to emerge from his hiding place among the old letters and parcels.

*

Royce sagged like a drunkard in the cold drizzle. The village shop had been ransacked, windows gutted to leave empty displays and pale shadows. Garden furniture outside the front of the shop was scattered and broken. Glass shards caught the light. He looked down by his feet at a human tooth among the glass; a molar with a bloody root. Instinctively, Royce pressed his tongue along his teeth. His gums ached.

He looked both ways down the street before he stepped into the shop, his knife like a useless toy in his brittle hand.

*

Rows of shelves and display units had been tipped over. Mould on the walls, below cobwebs in the high corners, all dry and wispy like the hair of corpses. The aisles were obstructed by broken things and smashed jars. There were animal droppings and torn newspapers on the floor. Plastic shopping baskets stacked in a corner. A fine coating of dust covered each surface. The grey daylight couldn't reach the back of the shop, so Royce swept the far walls with his torch and frowned at the unknown symbols and sigils painted in black upon them.

Looters had stripped the store. He guessed that other survivors had passed through the village, picking through the things left behind. There had been many refugees on the roads in the early days of the outbreak; those stranded on the mainland and left to die.

Aside from the man he'd seen killed a few days ago, he hadn't encountered any non-infected people for weeks.

He picked through the wreckage and found a small bottle of water behind a toppled display stand, and a tin of mushroom soup under the freezer full of rotting joints of meat sloshing in water. He hated mushroom soup, but it was tempered by the discovery of a tin of hot dogs hidden in one corner beneath a collapsed rack of DVDs. He kissed the tin with his dry scabbed lips. Meat and protein. How bad things were that a tin of processed sausages in brine elicited a wave of emotion strong enough to weaken his legs.

He opened the water and downed half of the bottle before he remembered to stop so he wouldn't get cramps in his stomach, which had shrunk from lack of food. He wiped his mouth with his sleeve, gasping at the sheer relief of the water over his arid tongue and around his mouth, numbing the torture of his raw throat.

He picked through the DVDs, trying to remember which of the films he had watched and which films he'd never see. A rotating book rack as tall as Royce was still upright, and he spun it slowly to view the covers of pulpy westerns, bodice-ripping romances, and science fiction romps about explorers visiting alien worlds.

Despite his perseverance and thoroughness amidst the ruins, there was no medicine or alcohol to be found. When he had finished, and crouched on the floor in a corner hidden from view of the doorway, he gathered his meagre findings. The mushroom soup, bottle of water, hot dogs, and a packet of prawn cocktail crisps forgotten at the bottom of an emptied multipack.

Far off in the distance, the screams of monsters drifted over the devastated land.

CHAPTER EIGHT

As the rain fell through the empty windowpanes and pooled on the floor, Royce went into the back rooms to look for more supplies. The corridor he walked through was narrow and smelled of rotting cardboard, and when he found the stock room he was disappointed by bare shelves and discarded food wrapping. A dried human turd in a far corner. An old radio that didn't work when he switched it on and turned the dial. He peered through the grease-clouded window out at the back of the property and saw a bony, shrivelled thing in a red jumper sprawled on the lawn.

He climbed the stairs in the dark, the torch in his hand the only light to peel shadows from the walls as he entered the flat above the shop. In the kitchen he pored through the cupboards. Drawers had been emptied onto the floor: useless household items, drawing pins and takeaway menus. Dark stains on the walls like healing bruises. The fridge was empty, and the plastic fruit in a bowl on the dining table looked good enough to eat. He considered, for a moment that took longer than it should have, scoffing the congealed animal fat collected in the dripping-tray under the George Foreman grill. He went through drawers until he found a box of paracetamol with the capsules still inside the blister packs, and he was so happy he would have cried if weren't so exhausted.

Photos of a middle-aged couple on a wall in the living room. No bodies in the flat, for which he was grateful, and no signs of violence, not even a smashed glass or plate. There were no signs of infestation. A cosy little abode. He imagined the couple running the shop together and spending their nights in the flat. It was a nice thought, but it waned quickly, and then he was thinking about how they might have died.

The living room window looked down on the empty street, and the rain, driven by the wind, lashed against the glass and pattered like fingers. He locked the door to the flat and closed the curtains over the windows. He lit one candle and walked to the bedroom, where he chased two paracetamol capsules with some water. Then he undressed and left his stinking clothes in a pile by the bed and slid under the dusty sheets, croaking and wheezing like an old man. Shivering so much that his teeth chattered. Inside him, the scrape and ache of joints against sockets. His dry bones.

*

He woke from a nightmare about the plague manifesting into human form and wearing the faces of his family, and it made him reluctant to leave the bed and the blankets wrapped around him. His skin was hot and clammy, but he shivered from the cold in his leaden, aching limbs, and the blood was pulsing quickly behind his face. His breath smelled like sewage. No inclination to move, so he stared at the ceiling until the room stopped swaying. The flat was cold and he was unsure if the sun had risen yet.

It was a struggle to move, but when his bladder was close to bursting he got to his feet with a blanket over his shoulders and went to find a bucket or vase to piss in. He thought about staying at the flat for a while as he closed his eyes against the swell of his brain in his skull and tottered on weak legs; put one hand against the wall to steady himself.

He vomited a thin gruel into the pot sloshing with his urine, wiped his mouth, and couldn't think of anywhere better to be in the last days of his dying species. Peering past the curtains at the ashen day and the dull sky he realised there was nothing out there for him, so he returned to the bed and lay under the blankets and sipped what water was left. He passed in and out of sleep, his temperature rising, and in a fever he thought he could hear his daughter gurgling in her cot while his wife played something mournful and slow on the piano they kept in one of the back rooms of their house.

Later, as he twisted and squirmed under the blankets and his eyes opened to the sound of his bones grinding in their sockets, he saw the television in the corner flicker into life. Noise and colour. He smiled woozily, his chin and lips damp with saliva, and caught glimpses of programmes from the time before the outbreak: *Match of the Day*, *Only Fools and Horses*, *Downton Abbey*, *EastEnders*, and an old episode of *Top of the Pops* in which Mick Jagger strutted across the stage blowing kisses like some broken, gangling marionette.

Then, finally, the BBC News on the first day of the outbreak. A pale newsreader in a crumpled suit. He looked scared and tired.

"There have been reports of disturbances in several cities across the country. Eyewitnesses state that members of the public are attacking other people in the streets. The Prime Minister is due to make an announcement in the next few minutes…"

Royce heard sirens and the panicked voice of his wife until the television died and left him in silence.

*

In his dreams they came to him all meek and mild and full of sadness, their skin like marble. Eyes like coal in their gaunt faces.

*

After two days in bed, he rose in the morning and stretched his sore, stiffened limbs. The crack of his bones under his skin, and the creak of muscle, tendons and gnarled sinew. His smell was ripe and pungent, steaming off the damp bits of him.

When he examined himself in the tall mirror his ribs were like thin shadows under his pale skin mottled with bruises and furrows. The sharp angles of bones suggested starvation. He was a gaunt, haunted creature, tired at being hunted. His beard was matted with dried spit, mucus and crumbs of food. The bottle by his bedside was empty, so he forced himself to scoop water from the toilet bowl and cup it into his mouth, and it was dripping from his chin as he drank and gagged. It tasted of chemicals. He barely kept it down, and it settled in the pit of his gut while he sat against the toilet groaning with his hands over his bloated stomach.

After he dressed he ate a jar of lemon curd baby food and thought about the days ahead. Suffering, fear, pain, desperation. A loneliness to stop his heart. Nothing for him in this blasted land of the plague. He found a plastic box of Lego behind the sofa – he guessed it might have been for grandchildren who had visited – and sat in the living room with blankets wrapped around him as he built colourful houses and blunt structures. When he finished and the box was empty, he stared at his shaking hands for a long time.

The Lego houses broke into pieces when he threw them against the opposite wall. Scattered on the carpet. Why was he alive? Why was he trying to survive? Instinct? Something innate within himself? Of course, there were ways of escaping, but he lacked the constitution for suicide. To take his own life was something he daydreamed about, but the reality was beyond him.

He climbed to his feet with the blankets still around him and searched the flat again, in case he had missed a hidden bottle of alcohol somewhere, but the flat was dry. He craved a few pints. A few tinnies. Anything to numb his brain for a while.

Then he had an idea, and it was so simple he was dismayed it hadn't occurred to him before.

CHAPTER NINE

Royce cupped his hands around his face and peered through the window at the front of the pub. Nothing moved inside. Motionless shadows, like patrons at the bar. Shades of old drinkers. The door was locked, and it wouldn't give when he pushed against it with his shoulder. He went around the back of the property. The car park was empty except for an abandoned Vauxhall with its tyres shredded, and a mound of charred bodies where crows picked at blackened faces and fingers. Skin seared from bones. A large rat crossed his path and vanished into the shadows of an empty garage. The rats had fed well since the outbreak.

Through a beer garden of long grass and wooden tables with parasols leaning askew. The top half of a skull in a bare flowerbed. A smoking shelter where drinkers used to nip outside for a quick cigarette.

The back door was ajar, and drifts of brown leaves had formed just beyond the threshold. The windows were intact. He stepped inside and closed the door behind him. A pool table to his right, cues scattered around it on the floor. A nub of blue chalk on a stool. The table was clear except for the white ball, which he picked up and turned in his hand. He'd been a member of his local pub's team less than a year ago.

THE LAST OUTPOST

A bittersweet memory. Good company, a few drinks, and lots of laughter. Usually a hangover the next morning. He'd been pretty good, too, once beating a man who played semi-pro.

Less than a year ago, the possibility of his current situation would have been laughable, something snatched from a horror film. He ran his hand over the green felt surface and it was like a tactual glimpse into a past he would have given anything to return to. He missed his old mates.

Royce placed the white ball back on the table then walked down the corridor past the toilets. A woman's purse on the floor. To his left was a doorway and when he stepped through it he was standing in the restaurant and he was relieved that nothing wet and twitching slumped at any of the tables. Places had been set. Napkins folded around cutlery. Set on the middle of each table was a small thin vase holding a dead flower.

In the bar, when he stood among the toppled stools, the familiar bittersweet smell of stale lager made him dizzy. Beer mats and smashed glasses. Coins on the floor. At one end of the room was a small area with a sofa, a fireplace and a standing bookshelf. This would have been his kind of drinking hole, back when monsters didn't exist.

The front door was bolted shut. Windows looked out at the silent street. His attention was drawn to the painting over the fireplace: hounds and riders chasing a fox across knuckled hills. Horseshoes pinned above the bar. Old tankards resting on shelves in small alcoves and inscribed with the names of long-dead men and local football heroes. Framed photos from almost one hundred years ago of farmhands resting from their work with jugs of cider. A black and white photo of a Highland terrier with '*RIP Walter 1978-1990*' scrawled underneath. Fantasy Football results pinned on an upright wooden beam. Dusty wheat sheaves and ancient blunt hand-scythes decorated the murky corners, and a widescreen television hung on the wall near the dead jukebox.

He stepped behind the bar. The bottles hanging on the optic brackets were empty, as were most of the bottles on the back bar. Drained bottles of vodka, whiskey, rum and port. Some had been smashed into glittering fragments. He breathed in the ghost-fumes of hard spirits. A full bottle of Cinzano. Sherry. Bottles of wine, orange juice, beer, lager, and Coke in the small fridges. Budweiser, Carlsberg, and Peroni. He licked his dry lips. All room temperature, but drinkable. He felt a little giddy, and his stomach filled with fluttering wings.

He tried the hand pumps but they were empty.

Stuck to the top edge of the mirror at the back of the bar were photos of patrons and regulars. Red-faced men raising their pints. Silent laughter from open mouths. A photo of a ginger cat sitting on the bar and cleaning its paws.

Underneath the bar were opened boxes of crisps, pork scratchings, and roasted peanuts. There had to be over fifty bags in total. His mouth watered and it was hard to resist opening a packet straight away, but then a scraping noise from the kitchen startled him from his daydream.

Knife in hand he stepped among the stainless steel worktops over the cold tiled floor. A deep metal sink filled with broken crockery. Dust everywhere. An old bloodstain on a wall. Scattered metal utensils. Dry pasta had spilled from a split-open bag and formed a small mound on the floor. Rat droppings around the legs of the worktops and the scratching of the rodents from unseen holes. The smell of old food and rot permeated the air. The kitchen was windowless, with the only light seeping into the room from the doorway to the bar. Royce pushed away the feeling that he was walking into a tomb he'd never emerge from. He switched on his torch and swept it around, pausing at the entrance to another room to the side. The scraping sound was coming from further into the kitchen, where the shadows were taller and dense like fluid. The scraping sound was coming from an opened walk-in fridge at the back of the room. He slowed, careful not to slip on dried puddles of tomato ketchup and mustard, and with his legs heavy and slow he stepped forward and aimed the torchlight at the dark creeping out of the open doorway.

Royce halted, and a low breath escaped from his mouth.

The smell was awful and choking. Shrivelled, festering fruit and vegetables on the floor. Spoiled meat and dairy. A tainted ripeness.

A figure was standing by the back wall of the fridge, its back to Royce, flanked by shelves of rotting food. He raised the torchlight until it settled on the hunched, shivering form of an old man.

"Christ," Royce whispered, afraid that if he had to turn and run, his legs would fail him.

The man wore only a pair of blue-and-white striped pyjama bottoms that reached just short of his ankles above his bare feet. Lank strands of grey hair hanging from the edges of his scalp. His naked back was covered with red pustules and squirming cilia, and his right arm, which ended at the point of a black, dripping claw, was withered and knotted. Mutated. The scraping sound was the black claw raking at the back wall, gouging at plaster and brick. The man turned around, and his face was a gaping cleft of scarlet veins, wet apertures and teeth squirming through membranes. A bloated stomach glistening in the light. The man exhaled through his ruined face and a wiry proboscis emerged from the ragged damp hole. Its tip opened to taste Royce's scent. The man's bloodshot eyes, so raw and bloodshot, regarded Royce with something like excitement. His shoulders shuddered. His mouth widened and more appendages emerged until his lower jaw was swarming with a breathing nest of writhing feelers.

THE LAST OUTPOST

Royce recognised what was left of the man's face from one of the photos at the bar, and he stepped back, the torchlight shaking in his hand. He tightened his grip around the knife and opened his mouth, but his tongue didn't move and his lips were as dry as sandpaper. No words.

The old man breathed in the air between them, taking in the smell of Royce's skin. After every inhalation, the man quivered and gasped.

Royce raised the knife.

The old man screamed towards him, all damp and shambling, bare feet slapping on the hard floor. Squirming sounds fell from the wound in his face. His arms thrashed.

Royce put his weight behind the door and slammed it shut; the man fell upon it shuddering and wheezing. Royce bolted the door and only stopped retreating when he backed into a worktop and knocked over a plastic jar of cutlery. The old man, visible through the small glass pane high in the door, was pawing and scraping on the metal, his eyes still set upon Royce, the things in his face pattering and slithering, leaving greasy smudges on the glass.

Royce pushed a heavy table against the door and walked away. He didn't look back.

*

He went back through the main bar and through a side door to a flight of stairs leading to the first floor.

The upstairs rooms were deserted: a living room, a small kitchen, two bedrooms and a bathroom with walls speckled with black mould. From a photo he found on the Welsh dresser he realised that the man in the kitchen had been the pub landlord. No sign of the man's wife, but there were two packed suitcases on the bed in the larger bedroom, and a handbag on the floor. On the dressing table mirror someone had written *I'm sorry* in red lipstick.

He found a double-barrelled shotgun and an army-issue metal ammunition box of twelve-bore cartridges concealed behind some musty jackets and coats at the back of the bedroom wardrobe. He pulled the shotgun from its zippered holdall and held it to his shoulder. The gun was heavy, cold and intimidating, and he swallowed as he looked down the barrel. Royce had never shot a gun in his life, except for when he was a boy and he spent a few errant afternoons with his best mate Pete Skipp shooting at tin cans with a 2.2 air rifle.

He placed the shotgun back in the holdall and hung it over his shoulder.

It was a relief to find no bodies. But when he checked the hamster cage upon a small table in one corner of the living room, there was a tiny husk of bones and white-orange fur hidden in a mound of hay. Royce's heart sank at the sight. The water bottle secured to the metal wire and the small bowl set upon the bottom of the cage were both empty. He imagined the poor little creature's last days, starving and dying of thirst. Had its tiny mind processed its fate?

Would *he* process it, when the time came?

Royce took a linen sheet from the back of the sofa and draped it over the cage.

*

There was no food in the flat, so he went downstairs and secured all the entrances to the pub, hauled bar furniture against the doors and closed the curtains. He taped the edges of the curtains to the walls so no light would be visible outside when he lit a candle. He did a circuit of the ground floor and checked everything twice. In the men's toilets the cigarette machine had been ripped from the wall, and he stepped around scattered coins on the floor. When he put his hand inside the metal and plastic wreck and fumbled around he pulled out a lone crumpled packet of Benson and Hedges left behind by whoever had looted the machine.

He passed the next few hours sat at the bar with a beer and a whiskey chaser, staring at the hollow face in the mirror looking back at him.

The shotgun was a temptation.

*

Night followed the fading of the light. No stars, no moon. Dark beyond darkness in the streets. The village was dead, and Royce wondered if anything still moved inside the abandoned houses. Flittering shadows fell and rose on the walls from the lone candle set upon a porcelain saucer on the bar. He took a bottle of whiskey, the candle, and the shotgun into the kitchen, and he set them down, save for the whiskey, which he swigged from as he sat on a cold worktop facing the barricaded fridge door. The whiskey spread warmth into his stomach and made the edges of his vision watery. His arms felt like cotton wool.

He looked at the glass pane set into the door, and he grinned when the infected man appeared. Blood and another paler fluid were smeared across the glass, and the man's awful face was little more than a suggested shape. The man turned his head and a lone bloodshot eye regarded Royce. Slow, weak scratching against the other side of the door. Royce nodded at him and raised the bottle in a silent toast, then drank deeply until his throat burned and he was gasping. He wiped his mouth with his sleeve and looked at the man. The monster behind the door. He could hear the man's breathing and the wet flopping of limbs.

"Your name was Stanley Evans," Royce said, his words slurred and slow. "Your wife was called Francine. I had a look at your last electricity bill. Hope you don't mind." He took another hit of the whiskey. The fumes were a comfort and reminded him of old friends. "But look at you now, Stanley.

Were you in the first wave of infected? The ones who fell down? Were you infected by a bite or a scratch?"

Stanley Evans didn't answer. There was only that eye, impassive and dark. He snorted through the hole in his face.

"What's it like to be infected? What's it like to be one of *them*? Is there some great revelation after infection? Do you discover the secrets of the universe? Do you remember who you were? Do you remember your old life? What do you see when you see me?"

No answer from beyond the door. Royce grunted and shook his head. His eyes stung and felt heavy, grinding in their sockets like marbles in metal.

"What are you?" He was talking to the plague now. The virus. The pestilence. "Where are you from? Did those titans in the sky bring you here and unleash you upon us? What're your long-term objectives? What's your endgame? What do you have planned for us?"

Just the low sound of rasping breaths scraping through black lungs. Stanley's eye never left Royce, and Royce felt himself scrutinized by something more immense than the host body trapped behind the steel door.

"Are you a hive mind?" Royce said. He drank again and whiskey trickled down his chin. He was close to tears. "Do you realise how much you've destroyed? You took everything. My family. My life. So many lives. Do you know what you've done?"

Again, no answer.

"Fuck you, then."

Royce threw the bottle and it shattered against the door. He grabbed the shotgun, which he had loaded earlier, and stood and stared at the door for a long time. His face was hot, clammy and damp. His heart a cacophony under his ribs.

The thing that used to be Stanley Evans retreated silently into the dark beyond the door.

*

The night and the following day were splintered memories.

A bottle always at his mouth. Shifted the barricade from the front door and pulled back the bolt. Turned the key in the lock. His hand shook around the doorknob. The sounds of the infected outside. A pack passing through the village. He wiped tears from his face and dared himself to open the door and step outside. To walk into the infected's waiting arms.

Smoking a cigarette and blowing the smoke through the broken barrel of the shotgun, like he'd seen the actor Jason Flemyng do in a film once. He giggled, and it was the closest to hysteria he had been since the days after his family died.

Slumped on the bar with empty crisp packets scattered around him. Ashtray full of cigarette ends. Staring at his hands until his eyes stung from not blinking.

Playing darts. Swaying as he stood at the oche. Examining the sharp tip of a dart, tempted to push it into his eye.

THE LAST OUTPOST

He vomited undigested food and alcohol into a bucket once used for donations to the local scout troop. Taste of bile and whiskey in his mouth, coating his teeth. Wiping his wet face and gasping on his hands and knees over the puddle of his own gruel-thin vomit.

Huddled on the sofa with his arms around his chest and his eyes squeezed shut. Saliva on his chin and lips. Rocking back and forth in an attempt to keep down the remaining contents of his stomach. A bottle of vodka had been tipped over, spilling across the floor.

He smashed a glass and picked up a small shard and ran it over his forearm just deep enough to mark the skin.

Kneeling on the floor with the shotgun barrel in his mouth, sobbing over the dead. Surrounded by empty bottles and glasses. Just one twitch of his finger on the trigger would be enough. The taste of metal and gun oil. A murmur in his throat, strangled and plaintive. A voice in his head goading him to spray the top of his head against the ceiling.

He closed his eyes and imagined endless fields of green and trees below a never-fading sun and a summer sky. Somewhere far away from the stinking rooms and hovels of his existence. No point in surviving if there was nothing to survive for, and this brought him the sort of acceptance that desperate, hopeless people feel before they throw themselves from bridges or high-rise windows.

He smiled around the shotgun barrel.

*

His finger paused on the trigger, an inch from ending it all. He opened his eyes and slowly withdrew the shotgun barrel from his mouth, and it clinked against his front teeth. He took his finger from the trigger and exhaled through a mouth that felt swollen and numb. His face was sore as though he'd been pawing at the skin under his eyes with his long, dirty nails.

He put the shotgun down and stared at his hands.

*

Royce dreamed of fun fairs and village fetes, seaside arcades and FA Cup Finals; doing the weekly shopping and feeding ducks at the park; a night in with a DVD and a bottle of wine.

He dreamed of being hunted by monsters, the last man in a tragic world.

*

The sound of an engine being turned over and failing to start woke him from the beer-stained table. The rattling grind of an ignition. Royce climbed to his feet, swaying and bleary-eyed, and went to a window and pulled back the duct tape that was sealing the curtains against the wall. He looked outside at the street coated in ashen shades of dusk.

CHAPTER TEN

By the time Royce stumbled into the street with the shotgun in his hands, the infected were emerging onto the street and one of them was already at the car, trying to open the locked driver's door to reach the old man behind the steering wheel. They came from between the houses and emerged from gardens of damp vegetation and dense grass, walking or crawling, sniffing at the air. Skulking in the shadows. Snorts and pitiful cries. Idiotic faces opening wide.

Royce called to the infected man by the car, and the man turned to face him, shoulders crooked and heaving, gibbering through a lipless mouth peeled back from his jagged teeth. He came at Royce in a quick walk with his hands flinching at his sides. Royce froze, planted his feet and raised the shotgun. Heart pounding in his ears, his hands slick as he fumbled with the stock against his shoulder.

The infected man shrieked, mouth full of black rot, and reached for him.

The shotgun roared before Royce realised he'd even pulled the trigger; the recoil pushed him backwards, his ears ringing. And when he looked down the barrel he saw the man flailing on the ground with one arm wrenched from its socket and hanging by a rope of gristly sinew. His right ear was a dripping flap of perforated skin and cartilage. His shoulder was mangled and bleeding.

Royce stepped back and turned to his left just as a teenage girl in torn leggings and a blood-stained t-shirt ran at him from that direction. Her face was a ruin of teeth, raw flesh and red spines. She was within five yards of Royce when he went to raise the shotgun and it bucked in his hands and obliterated her right knee. She collapsed and screamed, clawing at the air with wet hands.

Royce rushed to the car. The man looked up at him with moon-eyes, then turned away and resumed his attempts to start the engine.

"Open the door," Royce said. "Come with me. I can help you."

The old man ignored him and tried again to start the engine. Down the street, partly-shrouded by the growing mist, the infected were massing, drawn by the gunshots and the man's attempts to start the car. They had seen Royce.

"Get out of the car," he said to the man. "I won't hurt you, I promise. I'm a survivor, like you."

Again he turned the key in the ignition and the engine started with a coughing choke. The exhaust wheezed dryly and spat black smoke. The man revved the engine and didn't look at Royce even as he put the car into gear and it jerked forward and shook and lurched away from the pavement like something with broken insides. Royce stepped back and watched, open-mouthed, as the car picked up speed and rattled into the mist just as the infected emerged from within it, and ploughed through the screaming mass. The sound of bodies being thrown aside and broken.

And then the car was lost in the mist and the nightmare shapes of the swarming infected.

*

Royce stumbled towards the pub and the open doorway barely visible through the spreading mist. The light of the lone candle like a beacon. The infected were upon him like hungry ghosts.

A gasping face emerged barely two yards from him; an old man with the skin sore and lacerated around his mouth. A choking sound from his throat. Royce fell back, cried out, and swung the stock of the shotgun at the air, disturbing the mist around him. Hands pawed and grabbed at his clothes, and he pulled himself away from the snarling faces and spiny limbs reaching for him. The smell of filth and disease, fermentation and the stink of open sores. Fingers pulled at his coat, scratching at the fabric like blind beggars. Rattling breaths behind him, trampling feet and wet spluttering. Grunts and wails around him, as if he were lost in the middle of the swarm. Scrabbling claws. The creak of unfurling limbs and weeping stingers. Cries of hunger from the monsters in the mist. He stumbled away from a charred face vomiting black fluid through a torn mouth.

The pub was lost to him, and he fumbled with the spare cartridges in his pockets, swerving away from lurching shapes and shadows. The visibility was no further than the reach of his arms. The mist was freezing and obscured the sky and the buildings and the road ahead.

He stumbled in a straight line, lost and shivering, waiting for death in those abandoned streets.

*

Running through the streets, the screaming swarm behind him as the light was fading beyond the mist. He looked back, mute with the terror of slavering mouths closing upon him, kicking his legs and ignored the needling pain in his thighs and calves. His ankle, still not fully healed, throbbed as if swollen with poison. The bones of his chest were so frail he thought his ribcage would collapse if the riot of his heart quickened any more. He kept running as pains crept into his chest and a stitch formed in his side.

The mist thickened and curled around him, turning everything into grainy shadows. It smelled of stagnant water and tasted like mildew.

Howls of the infected drowned his heartbeat and the sound of his boots on the tarmac. He ran until his legs gave up on him and he tumbled to his knees by the side of the road on an unknown street, shuddering and gasping. He squatted against the side of a wrecked car and broke the shotgun barrel and emptied the spent cartridges into his lap. Then he fumbled for two of the spare rounds in his pocket, and his trembling hands struggled to load the gun. Finally, when he had closed the breech, he looked down the barrel into the swirling mist, shaking with adrenaline and the kind of fear that snapped minds if endured long enough. He thought that if some awful face emerged from the mist, his heart would stop. But nothing came out of the mist to claim him. He waited for a long time, his body slowly getting colder and his extremities numbing. It was too dangerous to return to the pub tonight, not with the infected roaming the streets.

He sagged, breathed out, and lowered the shotgun. He put one hand against the car to raise himself then started down the road. The mist billowed, touched by a sudden breeze, like fluid. Grainy and cloying. Dirty. Royce was jittery, breathing shallow mouthfuls past stiffened, dry lips. The mist whirled around his limbs, startled by his movements.

A wave of disorientation hit him. The streets all looked the same – ruined, cold and grey. Sounds echoed in the mist. Shapes glimpsed or imagined; a pair of pale white eyes melted away, and quick footfalls in every direction. Sounds twisted and thrown by the mist. Everything dulled to deathly shades.

He hurried along the street. Grit crackled under his boots. Buildings were looming dark shades. Muffled sobs of the infected, high-pitched and mournful. Thin, contorted forms flitted past his vision.

A sound came through the mist; something like a baby gurgling in its throat.

Royce sucked in cold air. Footsteps seemed to approach him then veer away at the last moment. His chest squeezed his heart. He thought he saw a man praying in the mist. Demented sounds.

Some of those sounds tried to tempt him out to them.

Something screeched behind him, and he turned, staring down the barrel. He fought the urge to run. A sudden epiphany that he would die out here; opened up and emptied out like a farm animal.

He stumbled away from the sound of something shuffling wetly and stood flat against a wall. He pawed slowly along the wall and slipped down a ginnel between two houses. Trampled through dead gardens in the half-light and emerged onto the next street. Shambling footsteps grew louder until their author appeared in the mist ahead of him and jerked its head towards him. Low grunts and sniffs. Royce trained the shotgun upon the figure now motionless apart from the dancing of bony fingers. A clicking in its throat, and when Royce saw its face he halted and held his breath.

The infected man was covered in dried mud and serous fluids. Most of his clothes were gone and his body was trembling and emaciated. The dark stain of his pubis below the curves of jutting rib bones. His eyes had been mauled from their sockets and the flesh of his face was shredded and swollen. His low damp breaths were strained and weak, and he stared in Royce's direction until something else distracted him and he lurched into the mist like a broken puppet manipulated by lengths of twine.

Royce kept moving, sweeping the mist with the shotgun, his fingers numb with cold. Further on, he saw an infected person crouched over a puddle lapping from the water. He couldn't tell, due to the warped mutations of its pallid, hairless body, if it was male or female. He moved past silently, the creature hidden again by the mist.

Further on he saw two red lights ahead. Tail lights. Patches of mist glowed red with them. He approached carefully. The car was slewed across the road, the driver's door open, interior lights revealing empty seats. The old man was gone. Mist swirled in the headlights. The engine wasn't running, but when he placed his hand upon the bonnet it was still warm. Royce tried the ignition, but gave up after four attempts. He followed spots of blood on the road, expecting with each step to discover the man sliced open and steaming in the cold air.

He came to an ambulance abandoned after it had mounted the kerb. A dead girl no older than ten years old sprawled with a hatchet embedded in the pulp of her face. The wail of infected pierced the mist from across streets and gardens, and the cries seemed never-ending in the echoing spaces of the dead village.

Royce entered the first house he found, a semi-detached with an opened front door. He moved slowly through the detritus of someone's old life, past mildewed walls and dust-furred surfaces. The ceiling creaked and was veined with dark fissures spreading out from above the glass lampshade. Royce didn't want to be under that when it came down. A leathery, dusty corpse splayed on the stairway, broken in unnatural angles, grimacing in the torchlight at its own reckoning.

Beyond the rise of the stairway, something small and quick skittered through the bedrooms then stopped, and although it was unseen, Royce imagined it listening in silence just as he was. Probably some nocturnal animal scavenging for food. Maybe a fox.

Royce didn't go upstairs.

He stepped past a smashed cabinet full of china plates commemorating royal weddings and coronations. A remote control for the television crunched beneath one boot. He entered the kitchen and stopped, appalled at the stench of something like the fungal corruption found in old drainage pipes.

In the high corner between two walls and the ceiling was something like a spider's nest large enough to contain an adult human. Grey and fleshy, held to the wall by strands of the same organic material, trembling with movement from something inside. A narrow slit appeared and Royce stepped back. The shotgun felt slippery in his hand. The nest bulged, split wide, and disgorged a blind, gasping thing which slopped onto the floor with its white limbs enfolded like a newborn foal. A phlegmy cough came from its mouth. It was human in shape, but its skin was mottled with grey and completely hairless. Its mouth yawned open. Razor maw. Born with teeth. Eyes the colour of flea eggs. Curved onyx claws at the end of stunted limbs.

This was something Royce hadn't seen before. Something new, born in a spill of filth and offal. The plague had imagination.

The creature sucked the dirty air into its lungs. Amniotic fluid dripped from its quivering body and pooled on the floor. An overwhelming stink of effluent filled the room. The creature raised itself onto four limbs, shedding the shredded remains of its amniotic sac. Membranes slipped to the floor. A quadrupedal nightmare. It turned towards Royce and sniffed the air; the scent of Royce's unwashed body, sweat and fear, excited the creature. Spools of fluid hanging from its abdomen.

The creature snapped its jaws together, clacking like dull ivory, keen for sustenance and meat, and jerked its head towards Royce. Lips pulled back from teeth. Legs straining, corded with thin muscle, ready to leap. Because it would leap and it would fall upon its prey.

It growled.

Royce raised the shotgun and its roar filled the house and mist beyond.

*

Out on the streets again and he ran in faltering strides. More scuffled footsteps from down the street. A narrow, man-like silhouette rose from behind a ruined car, paused as if to note how much meat was on him, and then dipped out of sight. Royce rubbed at his eyes. His arms throbbed.

A gibbering white thing on splayed legs scuttled across his line of sight before it was lost in the mist.

Royce staggered up the road, relying on a failing sense of direction. His breathing was too loud. He gritted his teeth. There was a light ahead, an orb of white light about the size of a golf ball.

He slowed. The light wavered. He started towards the light. It was nestled between a pile of rubbish bags and a crumbling wall. The light shimmered, as if immersed in water.

Royce was almost upon the light when it moved away to their right, as if dragged by an unseen reel, lost in the mist. Something moved from that direction with the sound of unfolding limbs. The rustling of fabric. The light had been bait upon a hair-like filament, and the creature lunged at him from between the wrecks of two cars, feverish eyes set with insane hunger. Below its mouth, the light blinkered strobe-like.

THE LAST OUTPOST

Royce staggered away as jaws snapped at the air where his head had been. Heat and rot-stink steamed off the monster. As he stumbled into the mist, Royce glanced back and caught a glimpse of the creature. It retained a man's shape but twisted and deformed. A bipedal, hunched form the colour of diseased meat. Palsied arms. Something awful created from the plague.

It roared as he fled.

Confused and disorientated, a fever of cold sweat upon him, he kept running, tensed for claws against the soft nape of his neck. He didn't want to die without seeing the sky one last time.

The mist formed shapes and writhed around him. His legs throbbed and pain lanced his knees with each footfall, and the rucksack slapped against his back. Iron fingers tightened round his lungs. Each breath was fought for and taken gratefully. He was running blind into the mist, gasping for air.

He halted at a junction and looked both ways. Ridiculously, Royce thought of Green Cross Code adverts on the telly when he was a boy. That bloke who was Darth Vader, but not the voice. To his right the mist shifted with the approaching shapes of running infected. Royce went the other way as a chorus of vile mouths shrieked behind him. He dodged a man with black tendrils sprouting from the cavity of his chest. The man's face was stretched and flushed with ecstasy as he fell to his knees and his eyes rolled back in their sockets.

Royce ran into a cul-de-sac and stumbled into a man in a torn shirt hanging in strips from his shoulders. The man lashed out at Royce with one deformed hand. More infected emerged to his left from the shadows of gardens. Royce ran for the house directly ahead, across the sodden lawn and gravel driveway, past a dead animal on the grass, and tried the front door but it was locked. He glanced back at the infected gaining upon him. He was shivering with cold and couldn't think for the sound of his heart.

As Royce raised the shotgun to shoot the lock, a little boy emerged from around the side of the house, on all fours and naked, sniffing at the long grass. He mewled lowly, his head jerking from side-to-side, his throat swollen with something that rippled against his marble skin. What remained of his hair was in ragged tufts.

Royce froze as the boy padded onto the basalt-coloured flowerbed of dead stalks. Steam rose from his scrawny body as he scrabbled in the dirt like a carrion beetle, an awful rattling coming from the wound of his mouth. The insides of his thighs were covered in shit and dirt. Royce glanced over his shoulder at the infected massing towards him.

The boy turned his head towards him and the rattling from his mouth became a prolonged growl through teeth no longer that of a little boy's. His face was little more than a Halloween mask of stretched skin upon sharp bones, and the skin flexed and flapped, then with a sickening heave, drew back from the lower half of his skull to reveal a maw busy with black wormlike things swaying and darting. The boy began to tremble as pale pincers burst from his flanks and stabbed at the air. Tusk-like and stained with red. He skittered towards Royce, his head caught in violent spasms.

Royce fired the shotgun as the boy reared up and shrieked. The top half of the boy's body became red mince and splintered bone, and what remained of him slumped on the lawn, legs still kicking. A nub of white spine against the grass. Pooling innards and smeared viscera. A young life released from the plague, and that was the only comfort to Royce as he stared at what was left of the boy for what seemed like minutes, but only seconds had passed.

The infected closed in. Royce raised the shotgun.

The door flew open under the buckshot. Royce dashed inside then closed the door, heaved a dining table against it and piled wooden chairs on top. The infected slammed into the door moments later. Royce emptied the used cartridges from the breech and reloaded. The last two cartridges, he realised; the remaining rounds were back at the pub.

The window over the sink smashed inwards and several blackened limbs grasped for purchase and clawed at the air.

Royce turned and started down the hallway towards the back of the house, but halted when the back door collapsed and more shrieking figures clambered through the opening, wretched and naked, bristling with spines and tendrils. A potent stench of rot and filth entered with them. A wave of flesh and splintered limbs. The children were the worst to look upon, and their sagging faces upset him.

Royce turned to the stairs and he climbed to the next floor just as the infected reached the foot of the stairway. It was one of the hardest physical things he had ever done to climb the stairs with the infected grabbing at his heels, and he only just reached the top step without collapsing.

Once he was on the landing he stopped and turned and fired down the stairs at the mangled things climbing towards him. In the writhing mass of limbs and mouths, bodies collapsed and thrashed into an unspooling mass, raking at the wall and the banister. So many terrible mouths all wet and mealy, gibbering and mewling.

Royce pulled down the length of string attached to the attic seal and a fold up ladder dropped. He climbed the steps then looked back. As he pulled up the ladder and began to close the seal, a shockingly-thin man skittered onto the landing, lowered his skeletal face to the floor and inhaled deeply.

CHAPTER ELEVEN

Royce waited in silence in the half-light of the windowless attic, crouching because the ceiling was barely tall enough for him to stand. He lit the cigarette lighter and its tiny flame animated his shadow. The infected haunted the rooms below, their insect-like clicking and whirring punctuated by the occasional grunt or bout of mournful lowing. They ran up and down the stairs, knocking and scratching at the walls, hunting him. Somewhere down there, glass smashed and there was a dull thump followed by a strangled bark. Claws scrabbling upon carpets and across the linoleum floor in the kitchen. A guttural scream sent shivers down the backs of his arms.

Later, as the night approached, the infected moved on in pursuit of other quarry.

*

Royce investigated the dark reaches of the attic, checking for other entrances. Cardboard boxes heaped against the sloping wall, filled with old Christmas decorations. The tarnished gleam of raggedy tinsel and scratched baubles. Royce felt a twinge in his chest when he looked upon the trinkets, recalling memories of previous Christmases and the opening of presents. The family dinner around the table at his parents' house. Bad jokes and party hats in the crackers. The Queen's speech and too much cake.

Royce searched the far end of the attic and found dusty paperback books from the Seventies; horror anthologies. A tealight with just enough of its wick to light some of the dark hours. Old vinyl records – Fleetwood Mac, David Bowie, The Cure, and New Order. A souvenir programme from the 1984 FA Cup Final. Children's toys packed into large Tupperware containers. He almost smiled when he pulled an Action Man – still clad in its British Army uniform – from underneath some old fraying curtains in a wicker basket. He wondered if all the real soldiers were dead by now.

Beyond the boxes, porcelain dolls with fixed grins and glazed eyes were half-emerged from a burlap sack, all gangly legs, and blunt paws for their hands. At first he had mistaken them for dead children. It was unnerving to look at them for any length of time.

Royce sat down and stared at the tealight's flame until its afterglow was imprinted upon his eyes. He heard the sounds of the infected above the creak of the house and the sighing attic walls around him. Royce tried to shut them out of his head. He took the old curtains from where they had been stored then sat and wrapped his body in the dusty fabric and closed his eyes. The flame burned out soon afterwards.

*

THE LAST OUTPOST

He woke in the dark, certain that the dolls had slipped from the burlap sack and were crawling towards him across the attic floor. He waited for the tickle of cold tiny fingers upon his limbs and the whisper of dust-dry voices in his ears, but they never came and after a few minutes in which his heart slowed to something normal, he was ashamed of his fear.

He stayed awake for a while and listened to the spiders inside the walls. Were they even aware of the human race's demise? Did they sense something was wrong? Would they care even if they did know?

He wondered what would happen to the ecosystem once the remaining survivors were killed or infected and there was only the infected left to claim the planet. He hadn't even considered the titans in the sky.

The world was full of monsters now. Creatures like that thing birthed in the house. He imagined the great landmarks of the world surrounded by hordes of infected and it depressed him so much that he felt sick and aching with despair. He thought he could smell his wife's perfume. Her scent. A great sense of loss washed over him and he blinked tears from his eyes.

The last thing he pictured in his mind before he fell asleep again was the Earth swarmed and covered by the plague and its progeny.

*

In the morning he descended from the attic and went out into the first light. There had been three bodies at the foot of the stairs and one crumpled, bloody cadaver halfway down, an infected man with the lower half of his face blasted away. Scattered teeth like forgotten marbles. The house had smelled of vinegar on the turn, and there were smears of stinking black fluid along the walls.

Outside, the remains of the boy Royce had killed were strewn about the lawn. Picked apart by scavengers during the night. A strip of red and orange on the horizon as the sun was rising above the curve of the Earth. The sky was clear, stars fading slowly. Dead stars, he thought, as he remembered his father telling him when he was younger.

The stars we see are already dead.

The thought of that interstellar distance so vast as to be incomprehensible. The notion had floored him then, and still inspired awe, even now.

He raised his head and stared at the vanishing constellations, those cosmic ghosts.

*

Ragged and nervous, Royce moved through the streets in the dawn. Nothing in the streets except wreckage and the bones of lost battles. He passed an infected woman hunched in the front seat of a Ford Escort. Her limp body hung out of the door, and when she saw him she dragged herself from the seat, but fell down, and Royce saw her right leg was bent the wrong way. She cried after him, her stomach bloated with something that made the skin ripple.

Royce didn't look back.

*

The pub appeared down the road just as the sun breached the horizon. Silence in the open and the shadowed gaps between buildings. Sloped roofs against the sky.

His head ached. Hunger pains in the pit of his stomach.

A young girl was feeding from the corpse of an infected man Royce had killed last night. She was no more than eight years old. Her mouth was all over the man's face, sucking skin and meat from the bone like a pig would dig for truffles with its snout, frenzied and awful. Human fat and grease were smeared around her mouth and chin. Her blonde hair was in pigtails but one of them had come undone into oily strands upon her shoulder, matted with dirt, soot and twigs. From her right shoulder to her left hip she wore a sash with *BIRTHDAY GIRL!* upon it. Glitter and cartoon stars. The skin of her face was sallow and loose as if it were a façade hiding her real face underneath. Idiot hunger in her eyes. The teeth in her little mouth were like shards of glass stained nicotine-yellow.

"You poor thing," Royce whispered. "I didn't know you ate your own dead."

He slipped into the pub through the doorway still open from last night and saw that his belongings were untouched where he had left them. And the relief was enough to make him dizzy and euphoric. He bagged what supplies he could carry, mainly crisps and drinks, and quietened his thirst with a bottle of water guzzled in one go. He collected the remaining shotgun shells and stuffed them in his pockets, then grabbed the last bottle of vodka from the bar.

In the kitchen, the infected man stared through the glass at Royce. He considered opening the door and killing him, but it would be a waste of ammunition. Best to leave him alone and hope he would starve to death at some point.

"Goodbye, Stanley," Royce said. "Be good."

He returned to the bar area and gathered his belongings, and he did so in a slow, miserable stupor because he knew that beyond the village and out into the grey land there was only a kingdom of rust and ruin where he would probably die hungry, cold and terrified.

His little empire of dust.

CHAPTER TWELVE

Royce didn't know why he was following the train track eastwards. There was no purpose. Maybe it was instinct of some sort. He would have spent some time pondering it, but it was irrelevant because he was very tired and all the philosophers were dead and gone.

He was hunched under the open sky, his breath white in the cold sunlight. Clouds made swift shadows upon the ground. Royce would occasionally study the sky, and when the cold air began to sting his eyes he lowered his face to the dull earth. He held the shotgun across his chest with the barrels pointed towards the ground. He was awkward and clumsy with the weapon; it didn't come naturally to him. His arms and shoulders still hurt.

The track ran parallel to a dark swollen river for a few miles until the river veered away to the west, towards the sea far beyond the horizon. There had been bodies in the water, and on his side of the riverbank he'd found a fishing rod left behind on the stony dirt, and a fold-up canvas seat Royce considered taking before he left it toppled and snagged in clumps of long grass, all mildewed and damp.

A pack of feral dogs crossed the tracks fifty yards ahead. Royce kept the shotgun trained upon them until they disappeared into the fields.

His heart broke for all the lost pets.

*

He stopped at a small train station just outside the village of Longley, climbed onto a platform and stepped around the mouldering body of a woman clutching a handbag to her plundered stomach. A small waiting room merged the two platforms. Dead flowers in the shallow troughs under the shattered windows. It would have been a quaint, picturesque place if it weren't for the signs of damage and violence.

He rifled through damp plastic bags piled upon a wooden bench, but found nothing of use. Royce examined a smashed Rolex he'd found by his feet. The hands had stopped at ten minutes past two. He tossed the watch onto the track. Then he opened the door to the waiting room and stepped inside.

The snack machine had been tipped over and ransacked a long time ago. Sheet metal ripped away from the frames. He crouched and reached inside it with his hand feeling for snacks and treats, but when he withdrew his hand there was only dust and a streak of grime on his fingers.

He broke into the ticket office, where a man in a blue blazer had slit his wrists in the corner by a filing cabinet, his head bowed to his chest. A skeletal thing with wisps of hair on a grey scalp. The knife, its blade crusted with dried blood, was still in the man's hand.

THE LAST OUTPOST

Royce found a small bag of Skittles behind the counter and then ate the sweets as he sat in a faux-leather seat, listening to the wind mourn along the empty tracks.

*

Royce crossed the track on the other side of the platform and climbed a grass embankment into a small car park. Makeshift shelters and ragged tents had been erected within a defensive square of parked cars.

Large scorch marks on the tarmac around the square. Soot stains and flecks of ash. Royce stood over the charred vestiges of dead infected and the sharp splinters of contorted bones.

They had used petrol bombs against the infected, but their last stand hadn't lasted long, and all that remained of them was scattered bones and mangled bits. Rats fled from the remains. There was nothing to be salvaged amongst the mess. Royce checked the cars, too, but it was a waste of time and he leaned against a battered Vauxhall Nova and rubbed at his face. He imagined the refugees' last hours holding off the infected until they were overwhelmed. Parents holding their children tightly. The last cries and screams and pleas for mercy. To see your family die and then follow them into death with your guts held in your hands.

He stared at a broken Barbie doll on the ground, poked it with one foot. Then turned towards the far side of the car park a hundred yards away when something large moved through the tall trees there and disturbed crows from the high branches. The birds cawed and dispersed. The sound of snapping sticks and the creak of branches pulled and pressed against. A creeping, distorted shape in the trees, without a proper form, like something made of smoke.

Royce made a low sound when the tip of a black tentacle broke from the cover of the skeletal boughs; then it was gone and he watched it recede and melt away, a shadow into shadows.

*

He moved through a park where the trees were like pagan effigies against a sky without colour, and abandoned next to the deserted playground was an ice cream van from which something raw and livid had crawled onto the grass and died in a tangled heap of red limbs and teeth. Beyond the park was a row of houses, where Royce picked through rooms thick with the stench of corruption. A family and its pet dog curled around one another in a living room still acrid with the smell of orangeade and weedkiller from empty glasses.

In a bedroom of the next house Royce found twin boys no more than six years old holding each other in death. Sinew, hair and bones in identical *Transformers* pyjamas. No clue as to what happened to their parents.

He spent the night in the living room of a red brick bungalow. Wrapped in a blanket on the floor, Royce passed in and out of sleep and imagined the faces of old work bosses looming over him and demanding to know why he'd clocked in late for his shift.

CHAPTER THIRTEEN

Daylight came from the east with the rise of birdsong in wild thickets. Royce walked for hours along roads and lanes and across fields of spreading weeds and dead crops. No more harvests and no more working in the fields. The countryside was silent.

He happened upon a petrol station just outside Glastonbury, and picked through the aisles for anything left behind by looters and scavengers. Loaves of bread reduced to mould specimens inside polythene bags. Behind the counter, Royce found a packet of mints, which he pocketed.

The fuel pumps were dry, and as he stood in the forecourt he heard approaching shrieks and feral cries from the south. He returned inside and hid in the aisles as a flock of infected passed through the forecourt and into the fields.

When the infected were gone, he re-emerged and carried on down the road, mindful of the crows circling overhead.

*

Where am I going?

He blew on his hands and rubbed them together as he walked, one foot after the other, and each step was another pointless movement. He looked at the sky. Looked at his shabby boots. Looked at the stones and the dead leaves on the worn tarmac, and the muddy slush at the side of the road.

Where are you going?

"I don't know."

You don't know.

"I don't know."

You'll die out here.

"Fuck off."

Overgrown nettles and brambles reached for him. Thorns snagged his coat and pulled him back, and he had to crouch and quieten his breathing when something tall with rasping breath thrashed through the undergrowth to his right several yards away. Something passing through. Royce had the impression of a thin-limbed thing slick with secretions. Then he stood and moved on.

Two miles further on, he had to hide in a ditch when he stumbled upon a pack of infected clawing and scraping at an embankment to burrow into the rabbit warrens within. He watched in disgust and fascination as the infected tore into the earth and pulled the terrified animals from their shelters and went at them with their black teeth and palsied hands. Their naked, twitching forms maggot-pale against the black dirt. The rabbits struggled and made little sounds as they were caught, their legs kicking until the fur and skin were peeled from their squirming bodies. Small joints, bones and skulls popped and snapped between busy mouths. Sinew and ligament split and stuffed into wet maws.

The infected fed well. Small bodies were left ravaged and steaming on the cold ground. Rubbery organs, fleshy valves and lumps. Offal and skulls. A feeding frenzy.

One of the infected, a woman in a cooking apron flapping about her shins, stumbled down and through the ditch barely ten yards from where Royce was hiding, her head nodding like a bulbous flesh-sac. With her splintered mouth she tore at a small mound of grey fur and meat all limp and hanging in her hands. Gnawing at the bones. Too absorbed in the dripping pelt to notice him. Royce watched her vanish into the fields like a pale shadow.

He slipped away into the darkening murk before the monsters stripped the warren clean and went hunting for larger prey.

*

Royce spent the night in the back of a wrecked Mercedes van by the roadside, crammed amongst building supplies and tools. Muttering to himself, he fell asleep to the smell of plaster and emulsion.

He dreamed the dreams of an exhausted man. The chambers of his mind revealed in his slumber. The infected haunted him, gave him no respite. Shuttered nightmares of heads jerking and nodding as the mouths within them babbled and gibbered ceaselessly.

THE LAST OUTPOST

And he was among a swarm of *them*, pulled and pushed within the pulsing mass of bodies, following the tide of their movements.

One mind. A whispering voice in the back of his skull. He looked around and saw people he once knew. Old friends he missed in the cold dark nights of his isolation, nothing in their eyes but animal hunger and the need to infect. The need to spread the plague and propagate, and make others like them.

Some of the infected continued to mutate around him: arms twisting into hooked appendages; faces splitting from chin to brow so that ponderous feelers could emerge and writhe; bones pushing against translucent skin, forming bodies into hunched, appalling positions. Black fluid wept from gnashing mouths. Swollen stomachs and sore lips pulled back from razor teeth. The stink of piss and dysentery. Many of the infected stood with their heads lowered as if in remembrance of their past lives; others stared at the black sky with their eyes bright and livid. A woman was hunched over with her hands worrying at her mouth, and there was something nasty between her teeth.

Royce noticed some of the infected still wore the torn remains of the uniforms from their old lives. Soldiers, police officers and nurses, paramedics, firemen and priests. A man chittering in the shredded rags of a mud-stained business suit.

Royce looked down at his feet and they were mired between slithering bodies that floundered and gasped and fed on each other with sucking mouths. There were children. He cried amongst them and tried to close his eyes but there were no lids to hide them, and when he clawed at his face the skin was like rice paper and it sloughed away to reveal his painted skull and the black hole now lipless and wet. Bones cracked in his limbs. He sobbed and wailed and thrashed as something from within a cosmic abyss spoke to him in a song of static, solar winds and black stars.

*

He woke to the slow creep of dawn and lay there for a while listening to blackbirds and sparrows in the hedgerows. Nature abides, he thought, and it brought him a note of comfort to know that birds would continue to sing and fly and raise their young in nests of small sticks, long after his death.

Royce spent the morning walking eastwards. Heavy rain swept the horizon to the north. He passed things in the road – a rain-sodden glove, a hubcap, a tennis ball. The pages of a celebrity gossip magazine flapped in a shallow puddle. He passed the fading shapes of villages, too fearful of what dwelled in those silent places.

Electrical appliances had been dumped on the flattened grass by the side of the road: a portable television, a microwave, a hairdryer. Burnt plastic and twisted wires in the pale yellow grass.

THE LAST OUTPOST

Drizzle began to fall, so Royce pulled the hood over his head and hid his face from the sky. Gravel and grit crackled under his feet. He stopped to tie his bootlaces and when he looked ahead, something by the side of the road caught his eye. The shape of a human form cowering in a tarp.

As Royce approached, he saw the suggestion of a face inside the thin hood.

The old man looked up at Royce. Solemn eyes ringed with grime above a grey scraggly beard. A man dwindling in the slow rain. There was a hatchet laid across his thighs.

Royce recognised him.

"We have to stop meeting like this," the old man said, shivering in the drizzle. He eyed the shotgun. His voice a tired murmur through a dry mouth.

Royce appraised him and the hatchet in silence. "You okay?"

"Living the high life. You?"

Royce looked both ways of the road, and for an ambush. "Moving around. Bit of sightseeing."

"I'm sorry about what happened, when I drove off and left you in the street with the infected. I panicked. I was scared." A tremor passed over his lips as he scratched one side of his mouth.

"Don't worry about it," Royce said.

"Really?"

"Yes."

"Okay."

"What are you doing here?" Royce said.

The old man sighed. A forlorn creature at the end of the world. "I don't know. I'm so tired. So tired." His head was nodding faintly. "Stopped here to rest. I think I fell asleep. Not sure. Not sure of anything. Are you real?"

"Just as real as you."

"Or maybe we're just the last imaginings of a dying race. Maybe we're just ghosts drifting along the road."

Royce stretched his neck and winced at the dull pain down his spine. He scanned the countryside around them, then back at the man. "Where were you heading?"

"Just walking the roads. Trying to avoid the infected. What about you?"

"The same."

"Can I come with you?"

Royce eyed the black tarmac stretching away through the low hills and rises.

"We should stick together," the old man said. "We could be the last two left alive."

"I'm not carrying any of your stuff," said Royce.

The man nodded and rose to his feet in his tattered trainers. A padded jacket and stained rucksack under the dripping tarp. He offered a grimy hand, and he smelled of wet hair and blocked drains. "I'm George. Pleased to meet you."

CHAPTER FOURTEEN

They kept to the roads as the drizzle turned to sleet in the biting cold. The wind ghosted through tree tops and stirred the long grass around the bases of the dripping trunks gnarled by age and winter.

"Have you seen anything in the skies?" George asked.

Royce watched the roadsides and the shadows beneath the trees. "Like what?"

"Planes or helicopters. Hot air balloons."

Royce glanced at him and frowned. "Nothing. Not since the first days of the outbreak."

"Have you seen any of those *things*? You know…those things in the clouds."

"Not very often."

"What do you think they are?"

"You ask a lot of questions, George."

"I'm making conversation."

"Is that what you're doing?"

"Yes."

"Fair enough."

"So…what do you think they are?"

Royce kicked at a stone and it bounded into a ditch. "I don't know what they are. Does it matter? We can't do anything about them. The plague has already done its worst."

George nodded at the sky. "They're from out there, somewhere. Beyond the stars."

"You know that for certain?"

"What else could they be?"

"I don't know."

George didn't speak for a while, and then he said, "Alien gods."

Royce looked at him. "Really?"

"Things beyond our comprehension, Royce. Entities that see us as insects to be destroyed or used for other purposes."

"So you think they unleashed the plague to eradicate us like we're a nest of insects?"

"Maybe. I don't know."

"You got any other theories?" Royce said.

"Spores," George said.

"What?"

"Those *things* released spores that infected the population. As far as we know, the plague hit worldwide in the space of a few hours. That's not a simple virus, Royce."

Royce scanned the fields, blinking at the sleet falling at his face. His arms were going numb. Nothing moved out there. "Sounds like some type of biological weapon."

"Exactly."

"Interesting theory."

"I know. I've got more."

"It doesn't matter," Royce said. "Do you think that rats wonder about how the exterminator kills them? Do aphids question the pesticide that destroys them?"

"I don't know," George said.

"It doesn't matter," said Royce. "None of that shit matters."

George said nothing and looked away. They walked in silence for the rest of the afternoon.

*

They found a building site on the outskirts of a village and sheltered for the night in a portacabin. The sleet became rain and fell heavily as the light was reduced to a sliver on the horizon and the desperate calls of the infected echoed from all directions.

Royce ate chocolate and wrapped the blanket tighter around his shoulders. He barely had the energy to work his jaw to chew the food before he swallowed it. George sat across from him, huddled with his back against the wall, scraping cold baked beans from a tin with a plastic fork. A candle between them, against the dark and the howling wind.

A desk and an office chair against the far wall, on which a calendar with a different topless model for each month hung. Charts and notices on a corkboard, and dry taps above a metal sink. A pile of high-vis vests in their polythene packets. A dead computer. Empty plastic cups still retained the faint scent of coffee.

"Do you think we're safe here?" George said between mouthfuls of beans.

"Safe enough," said Royce. "Better than spending the night on the road."

George looked at the ceiling, towards the sound of pelting rain. "I hope the infected catch their death in this weather."

*

Royce could hear the sheets of tarpaulin draped on the skeletal frames of the unfinished houses outside, flapping in the wind and rain.

George had finished the beans. He sipped from a bottle of water. "Do you realise that it's New Year's Eve tonight?"

Royce had lost track of the days. Conflated days and nights and unending hours. Darkness and light. "I had no idea. Fucking hell." He rubbed at his face and blew air through his mouth. "I even forgot about Christmas."

George was looking at his hand. "No presents under the tree this year."

"I used to love Christmas dinners," Royce said. "All the trimmings."

George nodded. "I should be at home with the missus, a good bottle of whiskey, and a Hitchcock film. That was our tradition on New Year's Eve." He looked at the floor and chewed on his bottom lip.

"Sounds nice," said Royce.

"It was. Yes, it was."

There was no talk for a while. The men listened to the rain.

*

At the start of the outbreak, George had been living in Exeter with his wife. The city had fallen to the infected within days and he had been among the first civilians transported to a refugee camp further south. The old man's voice was a small sound barely heard above the sound of the rain. He spoke matter-of-factly, as if reciting a list of plans and schemes. But Royce saw the pain in his eyes, the look of being haunted by the dead and the living. Royce recognised it from the times he had stared at his own reflection in the last few months.

"It was chaos," George said. "So many of the infected. They found the camp and attacked. The camp was overrun. The remaining soldiers abandoned the camp and left the surviving refugees to fend for themselves. Most were killed or infected. I escaped, barely, with a group of people. Some children. We hid, we ran, but in the end I was the last one left. Me. An old man. I managed to survive the following months by cowering in back rooms and the ruins of buildings."

"But you survived," said Royce.

"But I shouldn't have survived," George said. "And I'd give anything to die so that one of those children could live."

Royce looked at the shotgun nearby. "I know what you mean."

They talked about the possibility of other survivors and the end of their species. They talked about extinction.

"Part of me thinks this isn't real," said George. "How would we know? What is real? Someone once said to me that our reality is just a memory of a dream."

"Poetic," Royce said.

George removed his tattered trainers and filthy socks. The trainers were slowly coming apart. The skin of his feet was black with grime. Dirt under his toenails and callouses on his soles, dried skin flaking on his worn heels. The big toe of his right foot was swollen. George rubbed his feet and grimaced. The smell was awful, fecund and damp, putrid dairy. Royce watched George knead the pale flesh with his grubby fingers.

"Do you ever think much about the past?" said George, as his hands worked.

"Sometimes. More than I should."

"Why do you say that?"

"Because it's pointless. It doesn't help matters."

George covered his bare feet with a blanket. "It helps to remember the old world. To honour the dead and the lost things."

Royce shook his head. "Nostalgia's addictive. Once you start wrapping yourself in old memories you may as well sit down in the road and let the monsters take you."

*

Later, as rain lashed against their shelter, George checked his pocket watch and counted down to midnight, and when the hands struck twelve there was no celebration and no hope for the days ahead. Just a quiet acknowledgement between the two men.

Royce took the bottle of vodka from his bag and poured large measures into two chipped mugs he'd found in the cupboard under the sink.

"To absent friends," George said.

They tipped their mugs and drank to the New Year.

CHAPTER FIFTEEN

The first day of the year was much the same as the days before. The men had waited for a lull in the rain before they left the portacabin. Royce had found scratch marks on the outside of the door and footprints in the mud.

George was struggling in his deteriorating shoes, and he had to stop every few hundred yards to readjust them on his feet while Royce kept watch over the twisting roads and the dark slopes of land. He tried to pinpoint the distant calls and howls of the infected across the windswept countryside dulled in shades of iron and ochre.

Royce thought about his dreams the previous night, of dark matter and dying suns. He could remember his dreams with such clarity it was unnerving. And not for the first time that day he looked to the sky and felt weightless, tiny and insignificant.

"Do you think anyone else is out there?" George said. "Do you think we'll find someone else?"

"I wouldn't get your hopes up," said Royce. He cradled the shotgun in his aching arms. He spat. His nose was cold. The trees to the left of the road dripped rainwater from their black limbs. He saw a body tangled in a dense patch of weeds, its bare feet sticking out of the brush. There was a low, resonating wail from somewhere in the distance. Some kind of monster calling across the bare fields.

George shivered, pulled his collar closer to his neck. Royce shook his legs to quicken the blood inside them.

"Maybe we should've stayed at the building site," George said.

"No," said Royce. "I'm not going to sit on my arse in a fucking portacabin and wait to die. Better to keep moving, George."

"Why is it better? Where are we going?"

Royce sniffed, looked at the old man. "You asked to come with me, didn't you?"

"Yes, I know, but…"

"But what?"

"I don't know. I thought there'd be a shelter somewhere. A place to hide."

"Hiding places never stay hidden," said Royce. "The infected always find you. The only way to stay alive is to keep moving."

"What happens when you run out of hiding places, Royce?"

Watching the swaying trees, Royce said, "What happens to all prey, eventually."

"And that is…?"

"Capture and death, George."

*

A kestrel flitted above a field with its wings angled downwards and its head centred upon a spot on the ground below. The men watched when it dove and then rose seconds later with a wriggling shrew or mouse in its razor beak. George muttered something that sounded like an expression of admiration.

It rained heavily in the afternoon, and with the gutters and drains all blocked by the accumulation of several months' worth of leaves, wind-blown litter and detritus, the rainwater pooled on the roads and turned some into shallow rivers. The wind spat the rain into their faces, and George's feet were soaked because of the holes in his trainers, so they sheltered in the cab of an articulated lorry abandoned by the side of the road. Royce found a stash of crumpled porn magazines in the back of the cab under the fold-out bed. He laughed grimly at the women pouting in gynaecological poses and exaggerated, unlikely positions. Those faked expressions of lust and hunger. George glared at him as he flipped through the magazines. He put them away.

"If you're into that sort of thing, be my guest," George said. "I won't judge."

Royce put the magazines on the floor. "Seems ridiculous now."

George climbed onto the fold-out bed and lay down after taking off his wet coat, trainers and socks. He wrapped himself in his blanket and stared at the ceiling.

"I'll keep watch," Royce said.

"Thanks."

"No problem."

After a few minutes he glanced back at her and saw George was asleep. Then he reached down and picked up one of the magazines.

*

The rain had stopped and they were walking down the road, stepping around and over puddles and pools of water. A rainbow shimmered in the distance miles ahead.

Royce would not turn to look at George.

"It's okay," George said.

"No, it's not okay. It's embarrassing."

"I don't care," he said. "You shouldn't care."

"Well, I do."

"You were only wanking," said George. Royce groaned and shook his head. "Get over it, Royce. You're only human."

Royce's face burned in the cold air and his stomach cramped. He grumbled to himself. They walked on.

"Royce, our race could be close to extinction," George said, "and you're fretting because I caught you cracking one off. Don't worry about it."

Royce stopped and turned to him. "Don't tell me what to worry about, old man." His voice was harsher than he'd intended, and he saw George's eyes harden in the pale light. George pursed his mouth and was about to reply when his gaze moved past Royce's shoulder and stopped upon something in the field behind him.

"What's wrong?" Royce said.

George ignored him.

Royce turned to where George was staring.

About a hundred yards away, a female grizzly bear and her two cubs had emerged from the dark bracken at the edge of some woodland and were ambling across the field next to the road, moving in the opposite direction to Royce and George. George said something, but it was so mumbled that Royce couldn't make out the words, and he didn't ask him to repeat himself.

Royce watched the bears with something like awe and shock. They must have escaped, or had been released, from a zoo; a torn fence or a sympathetic zoo employee who'd opened the cages to give them a chance as the world burned.

The cubs pawed and nipped playfully at each other then, when they realised they'd fallen behind their mother, scampered across the waterlogged land after her. There was a shallow slash as long as Royce's arm through the shaggy hair along the mother's rippling flank, and her snout was stained dark red. She had fought something recently. Royce wondered what could have done that to her. The mother turned back to her cubs and made a deep, low, resonating sound to them that turned Royce's guts cold and made him want to hide in a ditch with his eyes squeezed shut.

Then, once the cubs had caught up, she stopped and lowered her large snout to the ground and sniffed at the dirt, swaying her head around as if to catch the scent of something nearby. Plumes of breath from her open mouth. Those teeth. The concave skull, so thick and powerful. Those jaws. A long mane atop the back of her neck. She must have weighed about five-hundred kilos, at a conservative estimate, and had to be over two metres long.

Royce and George crouched on the road and tried to peer through the low hedgerow hiding them from the field.

The bear snorted then huffed. The cubs could be heard complaining with little barks and mewls.

Royce heard George breathing behind him. Did the bear know they were there? As his stomach shrivelled and the backs of his legs began to ache from crouching, he waited for the bear to start towards them. This was how early humans had felt in those early millennia of tooth and claw. They had no chance of outrunning her, if it came down to that, and Royce didn't think the shotgun would stop her unless he shot her in the head at point blank range. But he didn't want to hurt her or make her cubs orphans. He had no wish to harm them.

He listened for snorting breaths and the pounding of large paws on the ground. Gritted his teeth, put the shotgun to his shoulder, his legs shaking, and stood.

The bears were moving away towards the end of the field, back the way Royce and George had come.

Within seconds they had disappeared into the trees, and it was easy to think he had merely imagined them. He stared in that direction for a long time after they were gone.

George stood and breathed out. They looked at each other. George appeared as relieved as he felt. He was gripping the hatchet.

"Makes you wonder what else is roaming around out here," George said.

CHAPTER SIXTEEN

They walked for another mile in the weak light until George had to stop and sit on the muddy grass verge to rest his feet. The sole of his left trainer was loose and flapping like an old gossip's tongue. He swore as he undid the laces and pulled the trainer from his foot. His socks were wet and filthy. His shoulders sagged. "That's just fucking great. Lucky I haven't caught trench foot yet."

"There are worse things to catch," said Royce.

George's eyes moved in their sockets towards Royce. "That's not much of a comfort."

"It wasn't meant to be." Royce stared down the road, where it disappeared under a canopy of trees overhanging from the rising embankments. He pulled the map from his pocket. "We're about two miles from the nearest town. We'll find some boots there. Hopefully."

George pulled off his sock, and his feet were blackened. Royce hadn't seen his own feet in over a month, too scared of what he might find.

"I thought you wanted to avoid the towns." George wrung water from his sock.

Royce checked the road both ways. "We haven't got much choice." He eyed George's foot. "Hopefully there won't be many infected there."

"Or bears."

*

George was resourceful; Royce had to admire him for that. George had taken a stained t-shirt from his rucksack and ripped it into three strips that he wrapped around his naked foot and then secured with duct tape from his pack until it was tight and secure, but not too tight that he couldn't wriggle his foot. He slipped his trainer back on and paced along a section of road until he felt comfortable enough to continue.

When he caught Royce watching him, he said, "I used to be in the Scouts."

"How long ago was that?"

"Why? How old do I look?"

"Old."

"That's funny," George said, but didn't laugh.

Royce scratched his beard and scanned around them, watching the fields and the hedgerows. "You sure the cloth and tape will hold until we find some boots?"

George turned his left foot from side-to-side. "Probably. I think I wrapped it a bit too tight, but it'll do."

"Good," said Royce. "Let's go. Only a few hours and it'll be dark."

They arrived at the town in the dwindling afternoon when spells of drizzle came and went and sometimes became sleet. Royce and George stopped on the road that led into the town, but as they looked around at the half-collapsed buildings, scarred roads, craters and sweeps of devastation, they realised there wasn't much left to call a town.

On the outskirts they had found the months'-old remains of several soldiers rotting and scattered near to a few rusted automatic rifles beyond use. Not much left of them but bones and the scraps of their distinctive uniforms. They had been dismembered in death.

"Oh my god," said George, his voice low and scraped from his throat. He closed his arms around his chest, his hand tightening on the hatchet grip.

After finding the soldiers, Royce expected to see bodies in the town, but there were none so far as he could see. Charred houses and the crumbling shells of buildings where water dripped through the shredded roofs. Exposed foundations and open basements flooded by rainwater. Toppled chimneys and crumbling mortar. Gardens reduced to piles of broken concrete, stone and earth. Bullet holes in walls from high-calibre rounds and rusting shell casings scattered like pennies. A yellowed spine and pelvic girdle were all that remained of some poor unfortunate. A Challenger tank half-buried in debris. Red brick fragments and melted plastic. Warped metal.

"Looks like they bombed the town," said George. "Smells like shit."

Where the street was buckled and damaged, the tarmac cracked and gaping, a sewer pipe was jutting from underground darkness, exposed and broken. Puddles of sludge and slopping piles.

Royce checked the ground under his feet, worried he would fall through the road.

Some houses had been almost scraped from the earth. Some of the streets had been levelled completely. The roads were buckled and gouged. Small craters filled with rainwater. The charred shells of vehicles. Water pipes had cracked open, flooding roads. Debris and wreckage strewn everywhere. Glittering shoals of shattered glass. Shades of iron and slag. Bones among the ruins, like little surprises for the keen eyed.

Tarmac had melted, re-solidified into ripples and then cracked, exposing the layers underneath.

The skin had been torn off of the town. It had been hollowed out. Royce raised his face to the sky and savoured the drizzle on his face. The town seemed lifeless apart from the scampering rats and the squabbling gangs of crows watching from atop walls and damaged buildings. Streets of rubble, smashed walls and torn metal. Streets that weren't streets anymore but long stretches of devastation. Cars with drivers incinerated to bone behind the wheels in the desolate silence. Burnt-out shops and pubs. Disfigured road signs to nameless streets, slanting roofs and haunted places. Collapsed street lights. Skittering things concealed by shadow.

THE LAST OUTPOST

Royce spat ash from his mouth. Gravelly bits of rubble and dirt trickled down a mound of broken stone and bricks. A blackened skeleton was sitting against the wheel of a heat-blasted car, showing off a sharp grin. The tyres had melted and reformed into solid puddles of black.

George's face was pale and anxious. His arms drooped at his sides.

"I'd heard that the RAF bombed population centres during the outbreak," said Royce.

"Desperate times," George muttered. "Bad times."

Ash and rainwater had formed a thick kind of slurry in the gutters. Royce noticed something bloody and furred crushed under some masonry. The town was an overwhelming sight. Bombed-out buildings wavered. The wind swept through what remained of the streets, and when he listened closely the wind gave a haunting wail. Trees were raggedy nightmare shapes of charcoal with arms spread towards the sky.

The sight of such devastation stole Royce's breath.

Churches, supermarkets, shops, a train station – all ravaged by ordnance and fire and battle; obliterated in some cases. Craters from artillery and mortar shells. A forgotten battlefield. Windswept desolation.

At least the destruction was done by conventional weapons; Royce had heard about cities in America and China rumoured to have been hit by nukes.

George scanned the street and beyond. "I don't think we'll find any boots here."

Royce kicked a small lump of brick and spat. "Keep an eye out for any infected."

They moved through the streets, avenues and cul-de-sacs like thieves, using the cover of rubble, crumbling walls and burnt-out cars. The ruined streets so cold in the late day, and no sound but the mourning ash-flecked wind. They passed a tall statue of some locally-renowned man dead since the nineteenth century. A landowner or politician, no doubt. It was pitted and scarred, and part of its face was missing. The name plaque on the plinth scraped bare. Further on they stalked past a church bereft of its spire. Fragments of stained glass caught the grey light.

More army vehicles wrecked and abandoned. The black bones of a small animal in a gutter. Fallen, smashed trees turned to drifts of charcoal. Grit between Royce's teeth when he opened his mouth. A tower block was blasted and tilting, its face sheared off, exposing the dark chambers of flats and abodes. Royce looked for movement up there, but didn't look for long because he was sure he'd seen a dead body seated at a dining table.

"There must be a high street," George said. "Shops. A mall. Must be something left."

Past overturned cars and a van resting on its side. A school was now a gathering of gutted buildings in which nothing dwelled but shadows and the echoes of children's feet in the playground.

THE LAST OUTPOST

The sounds of their movements seemed too loud in the dead silence and their footfalls echoed down what remained of back streets and roads blocked with sharp mounds of rubble and twisted metal. They skirted a crater that looked to have been made by an artillery shell. Water pooled at the bottom of the crater. Nearby, a skeletal hand poking from a mound of debris formed by the collapse of a wall. It was difficult to pick through the streets with so many obstructions and detritus littering the way.

Royce watched for ambushes in the narrow thoroughfares.

"I wonder how many people died here," said George. His face was slack and his eyes swollen in the bone sockets of his skull. Royce had never seen such devastation that wasn't on the television from some distant war-torn country or from black-and-white photos of bombed cities in World War Two.

George was first to notice the plume of dark grey smoke rising above the ragged rooftops ahead of them, serpentine against the sky.

*

Cars crammed onto the kerbs of the pavements and roads cluttered with debris. Royce and George halted fifty yards from a Victorian red-brick Baptist church which had escaped much of the damage wrought upon other buildings. But its exterior was scarred and smoke-stained and the decorative windows at the front of the building were broken. A canvas sign had come loose on one side and was hanging down the front of the church, above the open doors beyond a flight of wide stone steps: *CARPENTER FROM NAZARETH SEEKS JOINER*. There was no graveyard.

"Is that sign supposed to attract people?" Royce said, wiping his mouth.

"Not a fan?" said George.

Royce spat. "Never really bothered with any of that stuff. You?"

"I was a choir boy, a very long time ago. Church of England. Lots of repression and dodgy vicars. My parents were very religious. They wanted me to enter the church when I grew up."

"And did you?"

"No. My father was very disappointed. He came to terms with it eventually."

The street outside the front of the church was cluttered with abandoned cars slewed over both lanes of the road. The smoke was rising from the car park to the side of the church, obscured by blackened shrubs, bushes and a stone wall with a black iron gate blocking the entrance. Royce could smell the smoke and something else he couldn't identify, which was acrid and cloying in his lungs. They stopped at the car park wall and peered through the gateway. The wasted muscles in Royce's chest tightened. The smoke was rising from a burning pile of corpses. That smell he had recognised was human meat, gristle and skin cooking in the fire. The funeral mound was approximately six feet tall and the writhing flames reached another four feet into the air. Heat stirred the air. There was another pile of skeletal bodies on the tarmac, soon to be for the pyre.

Royce looked at George and shrugged.

A man appeared from behind the bonfire, pushing a wheelbarrow overladen with twisted limbs, dusty torsos and dry heads upon which ashen faces grimaced or grinned. A jumble of browned scalps visible within the scrum of bodies. The wheelbarrow wobbled in his hands and leaned to one side, almost toppling on a few occasions, before he set it down and put one hand to the small of his back and stiffened. He wiped his glistening forehead with one thin arm. He was very tall, clad in a navy blue boiler suit and running shoes. A handkerchief covering the lower half of his long face below a pair of goggles. His long black hair was tied into a ponytail reaching halfway down his back.

He unfurled his awkward arms, lifted a small corpse from the wheelbarrow and threw it onto the fire. Popping, cracking sounds reminded Royce of cereal in milk. He and George watched the man work. The dry cadavers took to the fire like kindling. His breath fogged in the air. And when he was finished the man took off his gloves and goggles, pulled the handkerchief past his mouth and over his chin, and wiped his face with a tissue from one pocket and tossed it into the fire. He could have been aged anywhere between forty and seventy.

Royce opened and inched through the gateway with George on his heels. When the man saw them crossing the tarmac towards him, he put down the water bottle he was drinking from and appraised them without reaction. No fear, surprise or suspicion in his face. His grey eyes clocked the shotgun in Royce's hands. Royce looked for any weapons tucked into the man's boiler suit or within his reach. George walked alongside Royce, wincing at each step. The duct tape and rags were unravelling from his foot as his trainer scraped across the ground.

They halted five yards from the man. Royce coughed smoke from his lungs and his eyes watered, and held the shotgun across his body to ensure that the man had a good look at it. The bonfire crackled and spat.

"Hello," the man said. He raised his hands and his eyes flicked towards the shotgun again. "There's no need for that here, my friends. I've just finished for the day." The man's voice was soft. His tongue darted out and scraped across his lower lip towards a cold sore at the corner of his mouth. "My name's Charlie. It's been a while since I've met any survivors. Pleased to meet you both."

"I'm Royce. This is George." He nodded his head sideways at the old man.

"George. Royce." The man seemed to taste the sound of their names in his mouth. He smiled thinly, as if self-conscious about his teeth.

"We saw the smoke," George said.

Charlie looked down at him and adjusted his gloves. "I'm laying these people to rest. It's what they deserve."

"Even the infected?" said George.

"Especially them. The fire purifies them."

"I see," Royce said flatly.

George looked at the fire then back to Charlie. "Aren't you worried that the infected will find you out here?"

"This town is clean. They don't come here anymore."

Royce scanned the road behind them, then the perimeter of the park. "You sure about that?"

Charlie put his gloves in his pocket. "As sure as I am of anything these days. Have you both been travelling?"

"That's right," said Royce, unwilling to add anything more.

"Where are you headed?"

"We're not sure yet," Royce said before George could answer. "Do you live here?"

"In the church," Charlie said. He must have noticed the doubt in Royce's face, and he smiled again. "It's perfectly safe inside, and even if the infected did return, the church is still fairly secure.

"Fairly?" Royce said.

"It's safe enough. Trust me." The tall man glanced at the sky. "It'll be dark soon. Would you both like to stay for the night? I haven't got any spare food, but you'll be safe. Better than sleeping on the floor in the shattered ruins of some house.

"Okay," Royce said. "But I'm keeping the shotgun with me."

"That's absolutely fine, my friend. Let's go inside. I have coffee."

"What about the fire?" George said.

Charlie smiled at him. "It's fine. Let it burn."

*

"This place was a shelter," Charlie said, as he spooned instant coffee into mugs. "In the beginning."

They sat around a cast-iron fire pit, in the light of glowing coals and embers. A warmth Royce could lose himself in. The heat against his hands and face, so welcome after walking in the cold and rain. His shrunken stomach was full and content after they had eaten food from their packs. They exchanged a few words during their meal, but the conversation was stilted and sparse. He had thought it ridiculous at the time; after the destruction of society, social awkwardness should have been a thing of the past.

Outside, the funeral pyre still burned. Royce could smell it.

The inside of the church had been stripped of everything suitable to feed the fire outside. All the wooden pews had been ripped from the floor and demolished, and were now no more than assorted piles of kindling. The starless sky was visible where a section of the roof had been ripped away during the fighting. The windows were boarded over by plywood. Charlie had wrapped a thick iron chain around the front doors and secured them with a large padlock. He placed the key in the breast pocket of his boiler suit. Royce hoped there was an exit at the back of the church, because he didn't want to be trapped inside the building if a swarm of infected broke down the doors or smashed down the blocked windows. He was wary of Charlie and he kept the shotgun close to hand.

Charlie boiled a pot of water over the fire and filled the mugs then added powdered milk and stirred it into the drink. The smell of the hot coffee made Royce's mouth water. He let himself close his eyes and imagine he was somewhere closer to home.

George was sitting across from Royce, huddled under a blanket. He warmed his bare feet by the fire while his trainers and socks dried in a stinking pile nearby with his and Royce's wet coats.

"Sorry I haven't got any sugar," Charlie said. "I ran out of it a few weeks ago." He handed out the coffee. Royce took his mug eagerly and held it close to his face and breathed in the rich aroma. He was salivating as he took the first sip, and it was good despite the fine scum of powdered milk floating on top.

Charlie blew on his coffee and made little ripples across its surface. He sat between Royce and George, sipping, his eyes ablaze from the embers reflected within them. George stared at the steam rising from his own mug. He looked mesmerised and close to tears. Such simple things for desperate souls at the end of it all.

Royce savoured the coffee with each mouthful. His chest and stomach filled with heat. Between the coffee and the fire, he hadn't been so warm in a long time, and he could have wept right there and then in the company of two strangers. And he wondered about how events had led him here, huddled around a meagre fire in the ruins of a church. Hiding from the darkness.

"Haven't seen anyone around here for weeks," said Charlie. "Not since the last group of people came through here."

"Other survivors?" said Royce.

"Just people passing through. Refugees on the roads."

"Did any of them say where they were going?"

"Nowhere specific," Charlie said. "Just looking for shelter."

"Have you been here since the outbreak?" Royce asked him.

"I've lived in this town since I was born." He finished his coffee and put it down on the floor, then looked at his creased hands before the fire. A scar ran along the back of his left hand. A wedding band on one finger.

"Why are you still here?" said George. "There's nothing left of the town."

Charlie glared at George, but then his eyes softened and he looked away. "I had a job to do. Once the fighting had finished and the town was bombed, there were bodies everywhere. Bits of bodies and blackened bones. I was the last one alive. There was no one else. And there was nowhere to go. If I had left with the small groups of refugees I would have died with them out in the countryside, so I collected the bodies and put them on the fires I'd made. I've made a lot of fires, my friends, and I've laid a lot bodies upon them, but now I've finished and my work is done, and I'm very, very tired."

"All those bodies," said George. He watched sparks escape the fire pit as Charlie stoked the embers with a brass poker.

"Such a task does things to a person," Charlie said. "Wears you down. Makes your bones ache. Gives you bad dreams."

"We all have bad dreams," said George, staring into his coffee.

Royce turned to Charlie. "You said this place was a shelter. What happened here?"

Charlie didn't take his eyes from the fire. "The same that happened everywhere else, I bet. The plague spread and the infected were gathering. Bad vibes, man. I came here when the army turned the church into a rescue shelter – there was just death and infection on the streets. Over two hundred refugees crammed in here without food, piss-all water and limited medical supplies. No organisation. It didn't take long to fall apart."

"The infected attacked the church?" George said.

Charlie shook his head. "We didn't need the infected to tear things apart – we did it ourselves."

"How do you mean?"

"Once the water ran out, things got worse, and people started fighting. And from there it descended into chaos. By then the town was a battleground and the damage was done. People fled into the countryside. I stayed and watched the infected overwhelm the army. Then the jets came and dropped their bombs. Now nothing lives here."

"Except you," said Royce.

Charlie picked a scrap of food from his teeth and flicked it away. "Except me."

"Bloody hell," said George, and he stared into the fire with Charlie. Royce looked at them both and finished the last dregs of coffee in his mug. He wrapped the blanket around his shoulders and inched towards the fire.

"What will you do now, Charlie?" George said. "Now you've finished your work here."

"Not much left to do," Charlie said. "I'm almost out of supplies."

"You could come with us."

"I can't leave this place."

"Why not?"

"I don't want to."

"There's nothing here," said George.

"Doesn't matter," Charlie said. "It's my home. I'd rather die here than out in the wasteland. There's no dignity in death out there."

"Do you think we'll die out there?" said Royce.

"Probably. You've done well to survive this long, but eventually you'll be in the wrong place at the wrong time, or you'll get so desperate that you'll take one risk too many, and that'll be it. I don't mean to be so blunt, but that's the way it is, my friends."

"Thanks for your honesty," said Royce.

"The world was full of lies and bullshit before the plague, and that world is gone. The least we can do is to be candid with each other."

George said nothing, and neither did Royce.

A while later Charlie asked them, "Where are you lads heading, anyway?"

Royce looked at George before answering. "We're just trying to find somewhere safe, like the others who passed through here. Hoping to find some semblance of organisation – other people and civilisation. If there is such a place."

"Civilisation is gone," Charlie said. "If what I was told is true."

"What were you told?" George said.

"One group that passed through told me that the remnants of the armed forces had scattered, and most of them had gone rogue. The refugee camps along the south coast had been destroyed by the infected. One man told me the Royal Marines had tried to evacuate refugees from Sidmouth, but most of the refugees were massacred on the beach before they could escape. No one knows what it's like in the Midlands or further north, and some refugees had been told to stay away from London."

"So it's basically all fucked, then," said Royce.

Charlie coughed and folded his arms. "There's Starling House a few miles from here. It's an old country house that was open to the public. They used to hold weddings in the grounds and such other crap. I heard it was used as a refugee shelter when the outbreak began. I don't know if it's still holding out. I doubt it, but there's always a chance. Might be worth checking out. Some of the refugee groups said they were heading there. Can't think of anywhere else around here."

"Do you really think people are still there?" said Royce. He was doubtful, but Charlie was local and he might know better.

Charlie spat into the fire, wiped his mouth. "I wouldn't get your hopes up. You're just as likely to walk into a swarm of infected."

No one said anything for a while. George bit on his lower lip, his eyes mournful in the small light of the flames. Charlie stared into the fire. Royce was exhausted. His eyes grew heavy and weary, and he yawned into one hand. The town was silent outside. No rain or wind to disturb the cold ruins in the night.

Charlie fell asleep soon after, wrapped in blankets and a sleeping bag, resting his head on a stained pillow upon the floor. He looked like a pagan king. George looked across the fire at Royce, and the light from the flickering flames did nothing to chase the paleness and grey shadows from the old man's face.

"What do you think?" George's voice was no higher than a whisper.

"Of what?" Royce said.

George shrugged and glanced around. "This…"

"I think we're safe here for tonight."

"Do you think Starling House is worth a shot?"

Royce rubbed at his tired eyes with his knuckles and yawned. All he wanted to do was sleep, despite the fear of the dreams that may come. "Maybe. I don't know. Are there any better options? Can you think of anywhere else we could go?"

George's mouth trembled into a weak smile. "We could stay here for a while."

"I don't think so, George."

"But Charlie said that there're no infected here."

"There's nothing here. We can't stay."

"What if there's nobody at Starling House?"

Royce sighed and rubbed his face. "I don't know. It's too late for all these sodding questions. I'm knackered. We'll discuss it in the morning."

Royce lay down and closed his eyes before George could reply.

CHAPTER SEVENTEEN

In the morning Royce woke to find George crouched over him.

"Get up, Royce. Get up."

Royce sat up and grabbed the knife tucked under his blanket. "Is it the infected?" His heart was beating so fast he couldn't concentrate.

George's face was slack and loose in the light coming through the church doorway. There was sweat on his brow and his mouth wouldn't keep still.

"It's Charlie."

Royce followed George outside to find Charlie lying on the front steps with wrists opened to the sky. A photo album on his lap showing photos of Charlie and a woman who must have been his wife. Royce looked away from the photos.

They stood either side of Charlie and looked down at him, the sky brightening from the east as the sun cleared the horizon. In Charlie's left hand was a penknife, its blade dirty with blood and small scraps of skin. There were little dots of blood on the steps.

"He killed himself as he watched the sunrise," George said. "I woke up and saw the doors were open, so I walked out here and found him like this. He's still warm."

"Fuck's sake," Royce said.

"Poor bastard." George folded his arms.

"Last night he said his work was done and there was nothing left to do."

"He left us some stuff," George said.

"What stuff?"

They returned inside. Near their drying coats was a small holdall containing two tins of peach slices, a pack of AAA batteries, two glow sticks, and a litre bottle of petrol.

"He must have prepared this as we slept," George said.

Royce picked up the holdall. "Charlie, you sneaky bastard."

*

Royce found two empty whiskey bottles in a back room and he tipped petrol into each of them until they were half-full, then he cut a section of Charlie's blanket into rags and stuffed them into the tops of the bottles.

"Molotov cocktails," George said. "Nice."

Royce nodded. "Poor man's grenade." He placed the bottles into his rucksack and wadded his blanket around them so they couldn't smash. Using more of Charlie's blanket, George applied new wrappings to his trainers and taped them tight.

They left Charlie on the steps with the photo album in his hands and his face towards the sky.

*

The town receded behind them as they walked past lines of broken down cars in the road. Royce turned back once as they moved away and regarded the fading shapes of the ruins and knew that it would never be rebuilt and within a decade nature would reclaim what remained of the town. The monuments of Man would be consumed. Royce imagined a world devoid of life, save for bacteria. Just the seasons, autumnal decay and dark winters followed by the green shoots of spring. And what would happen to the infected when there was no life left for them to assimilate? Would they die out and dissipate into spores to drift upon the solar winds until they found a new planet to infect?

The plague would go on. The plague would abide.

*

They walked for hours in the constant drizzle, and they stopped by the roadside when the sky cleared and the sun swept the earth so that the wet ground steamed in the new light. The road shimmered like a river of silver fish. A toppled electric pylon in the next field, all grey and slumped, the bones of a metal giant. Dead wires and the last structures of the old world. George sat on a gnarled tree stump and clutched at his ruined trainers, grimacing and blowing air from his cheeks. His mouth made painful shapes.

THE LAST OUTPOST

"You okay?" Royce said.

George pulled the trainers from his feet and squeezed the rainwater from what was left of them. "Splendid. How much further to this Starling House place?"

Royce checked the map then looked down the road flanked by fields and hedgerows. Ahead, the road curved to the left and vanished behind a large area of woodland where crows and magpies loitered in the treetops.

"A mile, maybe two," Royce said. He wiped a fleck of grit from his eye.

"I've had enough of walking," said George, and he rested his elbows on his thighs and held his head in his hands. "I used to love walking before all this happened." He took the water bottle from his pack and drank with his eyes closed.

Royce sipped from his own bottle and stared down the road, watching the steam rise from the fields. When he turned back to George, the old man was looking back the way they had come, his face caught in a frown.

Royce wiped his mouth. "What's wrong?"

George didn't look at him. "Thought I heard something behind us."

Royce could only see about fifty yards before the road was obscured by fields, dark thickets and wild scrubland. He saw no one. "What did you hear, George?"

"I'm not sure. Sounded like a motorbike engine. I think…"

"You sure you're not hearing things?"

"My wife said I had good hearing; it made up for my bad eyesight."

"But you don't wear glasses," said Royce.

George shrugged. "More fool me."

"Fuck's sake. Who would be on a motorbike out here?"

George watched the road. "I think we're being followed."

CHAPTER EIGHTEEN

They hunkered down in a wet ditch shadowed by hedgerow perpendicular to the road, hiding among long grass, weeds and stinging nettles. The ditch was deep enough to hide them amongst the smell of damp foliage and animal musk. They lay against the ground and peered over the rim of the ditch, parting stems of grass and thistles with their hands. Royce laid the shotgun across his arms and watched the road approximately fifty yards away and as empty as they had left it. The thorny hedgerow behind them would hide their silhouettes from anyone approaching.

And they waited.

The wind swept across the field and stirred the grass. Within minutes a figure appeared, walking slowly on the road. Tall and thin, wearing a hood over a baseball cap. It was a man. The hem of a long coat danced around his ankles. Tracksuit bottoms whose legs were streaked with dirt. He had a holdall strapped across his back, the straps of which dangled behind him. He was holding a bolt-action hunting rifle across his chest, the barrel pointing at the ground as he turned his head left and right.

"A scout," said Royce.

More people followed the scout. They walked upon the road and in the fields to either side of the road, clad in tattered coats and jackets, jeans and combat trousers. Woollen hats and peaked caps. Some of the men were bearded. Some wore dust masks or cloths over their mouths. Eyes within dirty faces, scanning the landscape. They moved in a loose, untidy formation, like a ragtag army with no enemy left to fight. Cradling rifles or crossbows or shotguns. Pistols in gloved hands. Lengths of steel pipe. One man with a thick ginger beard carried a baseball bat wrapped in barbed wire.

Royce counted more than two dozen of them.

"Who are they?" George said. He lowered his head below the rim of the ditch and made little hushed sounds through his open mouth. Royce watched the men.

"Bandits, maybe. Scavengers. I don't know."

There seemed to be no women amongst them. Then he looked away from the road to the other men approaching across the field. They were spread out, but Royce didn't think the spaces between them were wide enough for them to pass him and George without finding them. But if they tried to escape now, they'd be seen. Royce dropped down and looked at George, saw his own fear reflected in the old man's face.

George's hands were tight around the hatchet's rubber grip. "What do we do now?"

"Stay quiet," said Royce. "Stay down."

George's eyes were damp and his lips were dry. He looked like something that had dwelled in the ditch for months, surviving on insects and weeds. Royce flicked the shotgun's safety as the men's footfalls crept closer. Voices from the road. Someone laughed, and it made Royce's shoulders tremble. George kept his head down and looked at the ground. Insects crawled in the undergrowth around them.

The men in the field were no more than fifteen yards away now. Royce waited, counted the footfalls to the hurried beats of his heart. His teeth rattled. He swallowed down his dry throat. George was breathing hard through his nose, and his mouth was moving with silent words. Royce cringed as the nearest man drew closer, and he looked up when the man's shadow fell over him.

The man looked down at Royce and George. But when Royce looked into his face he realised that he was barely a man, in his late teens with a wispy beard of blonde hair, and shocked eyes widening at the sight of the two men cowering in the ditch. Ears too big for his head. His mouth opened and he raised the snub-nosed revolver from his side and pointed it at Royce. Royce brought up his shotgun. The boy's hand was shaking and his face was too pale against the sky.

There were voices behind the young man.

"Please let us go," Royce whispered. His voice was slow and tired.

The young man's throat worked. He hesitated, sniffed, looked from Royce to George and back again.

"Please," said Royce. "We're no trouble and we won't bother you."

The young man frowned. One side of his mouth moved. A glimmer of hesitation in his eyes.

"Over here!" he shouted, and a second later he fell back with his chest shredded by buckshot. He screamed, followed by a wet spluttering and then a horrible silence.

"Oh shit," Royce muttered, staring at the smoking barrel. "Oh holy fucking shit."

Then the ground around the ditch was chewed and kicked up by gunfire.

"We have to move," said Royce, "otherwise they'll flank us and trap us in the ditch." The old man said nothing. His eyes were wild and frantic. Bullets whipped over their heads into the hedgerow and beyond. Royce pulled George with him and they began crawling single file along the ditch. Dirt and scraps of bracken flew around them. George was whimpering. Royce coughed and spat as he crawled, his palms pierced by thorns and thistles, and his face scratched by sticks and brambles. Royce scrambled through a gap in the hedgerow and pulled George after him just as a section of the hedgerow disintegrated and something hot streaked past one side of Royce's head. He grabbed George and they ran for the woods across the field. There were shouts behind them. All the way to the woods Royce waited for a bullet in his back. George was crying. Royce looked back and saw some of the men crawling through the gap in the hedgerow; others had circumnavigated the hedgerow and were emerging into the field from the road.

Royce pushed George ahead of him and they fled into the woods.

*

Hunted through the trees, they struggled deeper into the woods. Royce couldn't hear the men, but he knew that they were following, and he knew they would catch up eventually because George was slowing down and slowing Royce with him.

The trees were thin and bare, the canopy sparse against the fading sky. The air was thick with the smell of rotting bark and mulch. Branches and trunks groaned in the wind. Rustling shapes in distant shadows. He remembered the bears that had escaped into the wild and wondered what else now roamed the countryside.

"Keep moving," said Royce, fighting for breath. George was wheezing and gasping, holding his stomach. They stumbled blindly. Royce blinked sweat from his eyes and wiped his face. His limbs were too heavy for the rest of him.

George tripped, fell, landed on his front, and Royce helped him up and they continued, Royce dragging the old man with him. He guessed they were heading in the direction of Starling House, but he wasn't sure because the trees looked all the same and his heart was pounding so hard he couldn't arrange his thoughts above it. All he could think about was staying ahead of the men hunting them.

From their right came a buzzing sound that Royce slowly realised was a motorbike engine. Coming through the trees towards them. Royce stopped, and George fell against him and they both stumbled against a tree.

The rider emerged from between scarred trunks, ten yards away. A man in a scuffed leather jacket and a black helmet with the visor up so that the man's eyes were visible. He stopped the bike and revved the engine as he saw Royce and George.

"Run!" said Royce, and pulled George along.

The rider came after them, adeptly weaving between the trees. Royce pushed George ahead then looked back and raised the shotgun, but the rider was upon them and the baton in his hand swiped Royce's legs from beneath him. Royce fell and the shotgun tumbled from his hands. George glanced back but kept moving. The rider swerved away, unable to reach George through the bracken, and vanished amidst the trees.

Royce stood and grabbed the shotgun. Throbbing pain in the backs of his knees where the rider had hit him. One of the low branches next to him exploded, and when he looked back he saw the men giving chase. More bullets whipped past his legs.

Royce ran.

THE LAST OUTPOST

*

The trees dwindled and the woods turned into open ground. Royce held George by the arm and urged him onwards. There were raised voices behind them, back through the trees. Royce risked a glance over his shoulder and saw flickers of movement past the thin trunks.

A sprawling grassland estate. At the top of a shallow slope Starling House was a dark shape against the fading sky.

"Nearly there," George muttered, and he hunched into a coughing fit, but there was no time to stop so Royce dragged him even as he hacked onto the ground. Royce gasped and clutched his side as a stitch formed under the skin. Breath given and taken through gritted teeth. Their feet dug into the ground as they started up the incline. Someone called from within the trees. A gunshot rang out and it almost stopped Royce's heart. His legs burned; the wasting muscles in his thighs felt tight enough to explode from the epidermis. He pushed George ahead of him and they approached the house, struggling and slipping up the slope, and when they reached the top, the mansion was before them with its windows dark and recessed, walls strangled with ivy. An overgrown lawn with crochet hoops. Topiary animals were slowly losing their shape. The men paused on the large gravel driveway and looked up at the top windows, looking for movement, for anything. For help. The oak front doors were shut. Royce prayed they weren't locked. The shotgun nearly fell from his hands and his legs felt like they were about to give way, but he stumbled towards the doors with George at his side. The old man was wheezing, bent over with his hands on his thighs. He spat and wiped his mouth.

Royce looked back down the slope and saw the first of the hunters emerge from the trees. He counted seven men, and there would be more behind them.

He wrenched the great doors open just as a bullet hit the wall close to his head and scraps of masonry flew at the side of his face. George cried out and ducked. They fell into the house as more bullets hit the outer wall and the doorframe with sharp cracks. With one last surge of effort, Royce turned back and slammed the doors shut, and then there was only the darkness.

The sound of their harsh breathing in the dark was panicked and scared. Royce felt for the cigarette lighter in his pockets but was startled when George switched on a torch from his rucksack and the light bloomed into his face.

"Sorry," George said, and his face was beyond pale in the torchlight. He lowered the torch to the floor. Their surroundings were revealed. Royce blinked and frowned as his eyes adjusted to the dark. He imagined the sound of the infected scrabbling across the floor to meet them, but as he raised the shotgun the only sound he heard was a baby crying for its mother somewhere in the deep folds of the house.

CHAPTER NINETEEN

"It can't be a baby," George whispered. His hands were shaking so badly he almost dropped the torch. Royce reloaded the shotgun and looked around, his eyes refusing to settle on any single point of their surroundings. They were in a large hallway with chandeliers hanging from the high ceilings, glimmering in the torchlight. A suit of armour from the Middle Ages mounted on a plinth. Oil paintings of lords, ladies and assorted gentry lined the walls. A portrait of a man in an officer's uniform from World War One, with an Irish setter sitting obediently by his legs. Family lines, old blood, deep history.

Mounted animal heads stared down at Royce. The torchlight returned some life to their eyes as it swept over them. Oak wainscoting, seasoned timber, musty carpets and ornamental rugs. Royce coughed at the dust in the air; it was like the inside of some old church unopened for decades. The dust agitated the lining of his throat and coated his teeth. He needed a drink.

The baby was crying, still.

Doors to other rooms lined the hallway. A stairway to darkened heights. George stood in the stairwell and aimed the torch upwards, but its beam couldn't pierce the darkness beyond the third floor.

THE LAST OUTPOST

"Let's go," Royce said. "The men will be here soon."

They moved deeper into the long hallway, which narrowed into a corridor where the walls were decorated with relief carvings of old battles. George held the torch over Royce's shoulder so it lit the way ahead. The torch was the only light. Their feet clacked on the wooden floor. Royce shouldered the shotgun and looked down the barrel. The torchlight made cruel, spidery shadows.

The single corridor slowly became a warren, and they were lost. Lightless spaces, like moving through the abandoned confines of an old ship.

"It can't be a baby," rasped George, his rank breath at the side of Royce's face. "It can't be. That's not possible."

They moved further into the house, following the torchlight and the baby's cries into the dark.

*

Minutes or hours had passed – time felt different inside the maze of corridors. Royce felt like they were falling back into the past when he took in their antique surroundings. He used the sleeve of his coat to mop the sweat from his face. They hurried along one of many pitch black corridors and narrow passageways. Some of the walls were covered in blooms of black fungi, slick and bulbous, glistening in the torchlight. The fungi seemed to tremble when the light drew too close to it, and Royce detected a subtle pulsing within the black corruption, as if there was something readying itself to emerge.

The baby's cries sounded closer. George was muttering something to himself – a prayer or poem, it didn't matter. His voice wavered. The floor became slippery with an oil-like fluid that smelled organic and faecal. Far behind them, the sound of the front doors being forced open echoed through the empty corridors they'd fled through. Royce and George looked back then carried on into the house. They turned a corner and were hit by the stench of something ripe and sickly putrid. It tainted the air and coated Royce's mouth as he inhaled; he closed his mouth and breathed through his nose. The baby's cries filled the corridor ahead of them. One of the doors was open. Royce didn't want to go any further, and when he looked at George's fear-stiffened face he saw the same reluctance and apprehension he felt. But there was no choice.

"Stay close, George," Royce whispered.

They crept forward until they reached the open door and looked inside the room at the thing that called to them.

Royce sagged against the doorframe, filled with shock, horror and despair. George stood frozen, his face slack, small sounds in his throat.

It was a bare room in which a glistening amalgamation of flesh bleated and babbled in the far corner. It finally stopped crying when the torchlight revealed its form.

"Oh god," George muttered.

Babies and infants had been melded and conjoined in the plague's vile blueprint for life. A horrific totem of twisted little bodies writhing and gasping, broken and contorted into obscene positions where their movements were puppet-like and slow. Glazed eyes and idiot mouths gaping open. Low moans and pitiful yelps. Wet skin tore in places and leaked ghastly fluids that preceded the birthing of new limbs with maws and pale eyes. Pustules and strands of flesh all shuddering in the light. Some of the bodies were without skin, half-submerged in the mass of limbs and wet flesh that almost reached the ceiling when it rose to its full height. Tentacles tore the translucent skin along its vertical flanks and emerged to push at the ceiling.

George backed against the opposite wall and opened his mouth, but all he could do was let out a strangled whimper that died in the stinking room. He seemed boneless and tragic, and there were tears in his eyes. Royce looked at the abomination; it possessed no legs or any other way to propel itself. It was stranded in this room, and he saw that parts of its vile, heart-breaking form were attached to the wall. Its maggot-white body rippled with tremors and pulled oxygen from the air using all of its stolen little mouths.

The younglings, trapped in a purgatory of disease and flesh, called out to the men. The eyes of the abomination settled upon Royce. Baby blue eyes. Tiny fingers feeling at the air. Squirming legs and coils of liver-coloured sinew. One of the eyes was livid with the agony of self-awareness. A living hell of meat and pain.

The floor was stained with meconium and small drifts of moulted skin. Some of those small arms reached for him and he remembered his daughter and how she used to grasp his finger and enclose it with it her hand. His heart sank and his legs seemed to unravel from beneath him, and then he was on the floor on his knees with the shotgun beside him because he could not withstand the sorrow and the pain any longer.

The abomination let out a high-pitched gurgle, spat from red apertures and shivering clefts. From underneath the creature's body, within epidermal folds, several thin tentacles emerged and sampled the air. Then they made for Royce, their blackened tips quivering and flailing, keen to taste him.

There were myriad voices of children in Royce's head, all of them calling for help and entwined with the cries of newborn babies.

Daddy. Mummy. Help me. Save me. It's dark and cold, and I'm alone. I can't hear you. I have bad dreams, Daddy. Help me, Daddy! Help me!

Royce screamed. He looked at the abomination, and he was forlorn and hollow. The thin strands of his mind started to break. He felt himself slipping away.

Save me, Daddy.

George threw a flaming petrol bomb at the abomination and it shattered upon its heaving body. A second of silence, petrol dripping from its skin, until it ignited and the creature burst into flames. It screamed and writhed as its body was consumed by the fire, limbs scraping against the walls and the floor, and some reached for Royce but George pulled him away and they retreated to the far wall out of the creature's reach.

Its tentacles retracted and curled up. Royce was crying. Part of him wanted to crawl to the creature and embrace it while it burned. The screams of dying children and babies filled his mind.

Royce came to some sense of lucidity when George slapped the shotgun into his hands. He looked at the old man and said nothing, because there was nothing to say while the abomination in the room behind them burned and screeched and died in flames. Smoke poured from the room. The fire would spread.

"Let's find a way out of this fucking house," said George.

Smoke followed them down the corridor. Royce's eyes were stinging and streaming. George was coughing. Within ten yards something came out of the dark ahead and opened itself to them with shaking hands. An awful, pale shape of a woman emaciated to the bone. Royce's finger jerked on the trigger, and there was thunder between the narrow walls. The woman fell back against the wall with the top of her cranium so much pulp and fluid. They hurried past her quivering remains.

The carpet was damp and mushy. Royce didn't look down, especially when something brittle snapped under his foot. They heard gunfire far behind them, near the front of the house, and a man's scream spilling along the receding walls.

In the frail torchlight, meandering figures emerged from recesses, nooks and stinking holes. Claws scratched on the floor. An excited chattering from the upper reaches of the great house. Screeching cries among a series of wooden thumps. A naked man twitched and murmured in a doorway, gnawing at his own fingers whilst nearby a woman's face erupted into a nest of pink spiky tendrils; she crouched in the weak edges of the torchlight and screamed.

Abhorrent forms gesticulating in the shadows. The stink of things dripping in grand hallways.

Down hallways and corridors. Panic and terror swam in Royce's head, leading him to hopelessness in the dark. Mind-numbing horror at the suggestion of cocooned bodies on the walls. Awful sounds echoed through the house, changing direction, rising and falling, growing louder and then dying away into whispers. A chorus of wet screams rose from deep within secret rooms.

More gunfire behind them. The hunters were fighting through the house. George shouted something unintelligible, and the ceiling seemed to fall towards them and the walls hemmed them in, as if the mansion were constricting. Murmuring shapes withdrew from the torchlight. Royce and George ran blindly down the corridors. The torchlight caught frenzied, mad faces. A glimpse of lumpy reddened skin and staring eyes. Things suspended from ceilings, reaching down with long arms. Staccato gunshots echoed around them. The hunters must have entered from another side of the house. Smoke was creeping through the corridors.

Something gangly and pale shambled from the smoky darkness and the shotgun roared in Royce's arms. A screech of pain and the creature stumbled away. Royce reloaded while George stared at where the creature had disappeared.

Twenty yards on, they halted when a man with a pistol appeared ahead of them. Blood spatter on his face. He was breathing hard. He raised the pistol, coughing into his other hand. "You fucking bastards. You shouldn't have run."

He barely closed his mouth when a tall shape emerged from the doorway behind and impaled him through the chest with some sort of black stinger that enlarged within his chest cavity and turned his screams into choking gasps. He dropped the pistol and grabbed the dagger-like appendage, and he looked down at the bits of himself on the floor as the creature behind him wrapped long pale hands around his face and dragged him through the doorway it had emerged from. As Royce and George ran past the doorway, they heard sucking sounds from within the room. Royce was glad for the darkness.

After running down a long corridor they emerged into another hallway. A broad floor of the finest wood. George inhaled sharply when the torchlight picked out several infected people kneeling on the floor, feeding on torn and crumpled bodies. Fresh kills. Blood on the floor, the smell of it like copper. One man, although badly injured, was still alive and pleading with the terrible faces surrounding him. They silenced his pleas when they tore into him, and he came apart in their hands like soft bread. A man was slowly being absorbed by something with multiple tendrils and mouths. Another unfortunate soul was being dragged up a stairway by a woman in a stained nightdress, who hissed at the torchlight that revealed the knotted veins under her face.

The inside of the house was filling with smoke. The air was getting warmer with the spreading of the fire.

The infected were too busy feeding to notice George light the last petrol bomb. And when he threw it amongst them, their cries as they burned and jittered on the floor would not be forgotten.

*

"We have to find a window," Royce said. "Some way to get out of here."

"We're lost," said George. "This place is going to burn down with us inside."

Down more corridors and through stately rooms. A huge kitchen where bones mouldered on the floor. The sounds of raking claws and gunfire. Royce led George down a passageway that smelled of brine and raw meat. He was sure they were near the back of the house; there was a draught on his face.

"Nearly there," Royce said. He was breathing hard. His legs felt like heat and pain.

They halted when a bloodied man stumbled towards them. One of the hunters. A bite mark glistened on his neck. The man saw them and grimaced, raised his hands as if in surrender.

Royce raised the shotgun and centred it on the man's chest.

"He sent us after you," the man said. His voice was wet and he slurred his words. "He said you can't be allowed to escape after what you did to Matthew. And look what happened to us…" He took the hand from his neck and looked at the blood on his fingers. "I won't become one of the monsters. The plague will not have me. I won't let it."

Royce noticed that the man's right hand was enclosed around a small object. The man saw Royce notice and grinned.

"Too late," he said, and put his hands together.

He pulled the pin from the grenade.

*

Royce found himself among the swarm of thrashing bodies. The infected roared at the sky. There were bones on the ground. Small bones. And they were being trampled and broken by the feet of the infected.

A blood red sun rose over a spiked horizon of ruined cities. The infected looked to the sky, and the sky answered them.

*

Royce came to in the dark with the sounds of gunfire, screams and howling shrieks around him. He felt dusty and shrivelled, a dried out cadaver in a museum tomb. There was no breath in him and his limbs gave him agony when he tried to move.

George crouched over him, eyes manic and starkly white inside a face filthy with dust and smoke. His nose was bloodied and the blood had dried above his upper lip. "You hit your head pretty nasty when the grenade went off. I was worried you wouldn't wake up."

Royce turned onto his side and vomited on the grass. Then he lay back and squeezed his eyes shut. He remembered the hunter pulling the pin from the grenade and the shotgun bucking in his hands. The hunter died without a face, but the grenade rolled from his hand and rested against the wall. Royce had pushed George into a nearby room and followed, as the grenade detonated in the passageway.

He checked his stomach and chest for shrapnel wounds. Then his groin. He was intact.

"We were lucky," said George.

"Where are we? How long have we been here?"

"We lost the daylight."

"What?"

"Take it easy, Royce. You might have concussion."

Royce pulled himself up and sat with his back against a tree. He looked around. They were hidden in the treeline to the side of the house, and through the trees he saw Starling House aflame, fire reaching from its shattered windows. There were crashing sounds of collapsing rooms from within. In the night, the only light was the fire that revealed the area around the house where figures fought and died. Pops and cracks of gunfire. The surviving hunters were retreating into the darkness, chased by the screaming infected. Gradually the gunfire dwindled and the last of the screams echoed into the sky, and then the grounds were empty except for the bodies on the grass. Some were still moving. Wounded infected, many with severe mutilations and burns, picked through the remains and fed on the scraps.

Royce looked around at the ground. He looked at George. "Where's all our stuff? Our rucksacks? The shotgun?"

George wiped his mouth. The light from the flames painted his eyes. "It's all gone. Left behind in the house. Didn't have time. I was too busy dragging you outside on your arse."

Panic opened the pit of Royce's stomach. His heart jumped. He felt like he was going to throw up again.

"Everything's gone? My rucksack's got important things in it. Family things. My daughter's…" He stopped talking and looked at his lap, and in that moment of quiet despair Royce tried to remember his daughter's face.

With some effort he rose to his feet and staggered from the trees. Glowing sparks and flecks of ash drifted in the breeze. Smoke obscured the distance. The fire reached towards the sky. And when Royce reached the house he slumped to his knees before the inferno, whispering his wife and daughter's names to the blackened ground.

CHAPTER TWENTY

George walked among the headstones with flowers in his hands. The ground was soft after the previous night's rainfall and the trees at the far corner of the churchyard were bare and coal-black. Inside the church behind him, the congregation at Sunday Service were singing hymns. He hummed the tune of All Things Bright and Beautiful *under his breath as he halted by his wife's resting place and crouched next to the grave. The flowers from last week were already desiccated and brittle, and when he touched the petals with his finger they crumbled like ash.*

He replaced the flowers and said a few words to his wife. He missed her deeply, and her absence was especially difficult at night, but it was tempered by the relief that her suffering was over and there was no more pain to be endured. To spend another day by her bedside as she withered and cried would have killed him. And he wondered, as he had done many times in his long life, when his time would come to let go of this horrid, beautiful world and the loved ones he would leave behind.

When he rose from the graveside, the congregation had stopped singing, and he could faintly hear the reverend's voice delivering some sermon or supposed sliver of wisdom. Out on the main road, a police car raced past the churchyard with its blue lights flashing and its siren screaming so loud it quickened George's heart and sent a spike of adrenaline into his veins. He blinked in the grey light and looked at the ground. His shoes needed a polish and his trousers were frayed at their hems. He felt like he didn't belong in the world.

He looked up, startled, when someone screamed from inside the church, and he turned towards it as another followed. Both screams were silenced by something that sounded like the shriek of a wild animal.

George approached the side of the church, the dead flowers still in one hand. When he was twenty yards from the church entrance he halted as the doors flew open and several people burst outside, tripping and stumbling, screaming or crying. They fled down the stone path that led to the car park. Some of them had been bleeding.

Looked like bite marks.

Another scream from inside the church made George drop the flowers; he hurried to the entrance, only remembering to slow down at the last second. He paused at the threshold and peered inside. A few candles were alight, but the number of shadows made him reluctant to enter. He was aware, distantly, of a short concussion far behind him from the city centre.

"Hello?" he said, his voice low and unsure. He could feel the bacteria crawling in his guts. His empty hands grasped the air.

No one answered him.

Breathing deeply, he stepped inside and turned an immediate corner. He saw the pews, and the things upon them. The remains of the congregation.

George moved to the aisle, his eyes flitting in every direction. A man was slumped on a pew to his right. Part of his throat was gone, and the front of his shirt was bloody. The skin, and the flesh underneath, had been torn away. His eyes were slack and open.

Blood on the stone floor and the carpet that ran down the aisle. The smell of opened bodies. A woman lay to one side of the aisle, the left side of her face missing its skin and muscle. The left eye had been taken; the right seemed to regard him accusingly.

Why didn't you save me?

There were more bodies on the floor, savaged and crippled.

Why didn't you help us?

Before he could form an answer, he looked up towards the front of the pews as a dark shape rose from behind them. It was half-lit by the bleached light from the stained windows and the little flames of candles, and George stepped back, almost tripping on the carpet. He realised, in the poor light, that the shape was Reverend Booth. The man was staring at George. His mouth looked dirty and his body moved in spasms under his garments.

Something was wrong with his face.

George froze.

Reverend Booth was breathing hard, his chest shuddering, and he made a low clicking sound in his throat. George took another step back and raised his hands outwards. His heart was a swollen muscle that would not calm itself.

Somewhere in the city, maybe a few streets away, there was a popping sound like a firework going off.

Reverend Booth opened his mouth and his teeth were black with the blood of his flock.

*

George woke to thunder high above the house. Rain patted at the windows. He rubbed at his face with cold hands and cleared his throat, then rose from the sofa and shrugged the blankets from his shoulders. After lighting a candle he walked a circuit of the ground floor, checking windows and doors. Everything was secure, as well as he could make it, and there had been no visitors in the night. He breathed in the dust disturbed by his slow movements through the house, and pulled his threadbare jacket tighter over the grimy fleece insulating him against the worst of the cold. Yet his bones were never warm and he wasn't sure if he'd ever see the sun again or the pleasure of a summer's day, watching the cricket with a pint of ale.

George pulled the revolver from his pocket and checked the rounds in the cylinder. He knew how many bullets remained, but did so anyway, just to reassure himself. Then he checked the time on his pocket watch, and with the sleeve of his jacket he cleaned its glass face.

He went to the window above the kitchen sink, pulled back the curtains and peered between the wooden slats he'd used to reinforce the glass. Nothing out there but rain and desolate fields, with no sight of the sky. He'd been hoping to see some birds this soon after dawn.

There was a scratching at the exterior of the front door, like a dog begging to be let into the house.

THE LAST OUTPOST

George froze and watched the door, and he had to hold one hand against the edge of the sink to steady himself. The weight of the revolver like a stone in his pocket. His skin crawled at a low noise from outside, something akin to the bleating of an animal.

He stared at the front door for a long time until the scratching stopped and the only sound was the rain.

*

After a meagre breakfast and his daily inventory of the supplies, George climbed the stairs with a plastic cup of water and a small bowl of cold baked beans. Through the window on the landing, the stairway wall held the shadows of rain droplets on the glass. He walked to the door on the left of the landing and knocked twice, and when there was no answer he opened the door and stepped inside.

The room was washed in grim daylight from the window, and sparsely furnished, with only a small table beside the bed and a wooden chair near the door. In the corner of the room, where the walls met, Royce was sitting on the bed with thin blankets wrapped around him. Below the hood of his stinking coat, his eyes moved towards George, without visible emotion. His face, long-bearded, filthy and despondent, was like a poorly-realised charcoal sketch. The room stank of body odour and piss, old food and bad breath. Cracked walls mottled with human grease and damp stains, the wallpaper curling where it met the skirting board, and the carpet was more grime than anything else. The smell in the air made George want to clear his throat.

"I know you've got the revolver in your pocket," said Royce. His voice startled George. "Would you shoot me if I attacked you? Are you scared of me?"

"I've got your breakfast," George said, and he laid the tray on the bedside table. Royce looked at the tray then at George. His expression didn't change. When Royce's mouth moved and he showed his teeth George thought he could hear his lips crack and split.

"I'm not hungry," said Royce.

"You have to eat. At least drink the water." George offered the cup to Royce who, after a moment of deliberation in which he wiped his mouth and stared at George, took the water and sipped.

"Thank you." Royce moved the cup from his mouth and dipped one finger into the water, and when he raised it he watched the water drip from his finger back into the cup. "You don't need to keep checking on me."

"I'm not. But I worry about your state of mind."

Royce let out a hoarse laugh. George stepped back.

"My state of mind," said Royce, and sniffed sharply. "How's your state of mind, George? How are you feeling? How could anyone who's survived so far be *sound of mind?* Think of the things you've seen, and had to do, just to survive. Only the insane are left. So what does that make you, George?"

George didn't answer.

Royce appraised him then sank a mouthful of water. His chin dipped towards his chest.

"Anything else I can get you?" George said.

Royce was staring at his hands held upturned towards his face. "I have nothing left."

George hesitated, went to sit on the edge of the bed but thought better of it. "I'm sorry about what happened back at Starling House."

"You left my things behind."

"I saved your life."

"I had already saved yours. You should have left me there. I have nothing to remember them by. My photos, the plaster cast of my daughter's hand – all the other things – are gone. Lost in the fire."

"I'm sorry," said George.

Royce's eyes were moist. One side of his mouth quivered. "I can barely remember what they look like, George. They're fading. I'm losing the memories of them. They'll be gone soon, and there'll be nothing but empty faces and strangers' voices when I think of them."

George didn't know what to say because he knew deep down Royce was right. And this begged a question: how long would it be before he came to the same realisation about himself? How long would it be before he sat at the kitchen table and put the revolver in his mouth?

He couldn't look at Royce's face. "I'll leave the beans here, in case you get hungry."

Royce turned towards the wall. George left the room and went downstairs. The rain was receding, but the wind moved inside the walls. He sat at the kitchen table, placed the revolver before him, and covered his face with his hands.

CHAPTER TWENTY-ONE

In the days that followed, George kept watch and noted their dwindling supplies. He and Royce had been lucky after they'd fled the inferno of Starling House and found the farmhouse; the doors had been locked, but George had gained entry through a back window. Inside, the farmhouse had been untouched by refugees and scavengers. The owners must have left at the beginning of the outbreak, hoping to be evacuated from the mainland. George often wondered, especially in the dark hours, what had become of them, and every time he realised it was better not to know.

There had been some tins of food left in the cupboards; a few bottles of water, lemonade, and Coke too, but there was only enough left for a few more days at most, and the nearest village was four miles away. He had become used to the hunger pangs and cravings, but he knew they would eventually run out of food and he would have to leave the house to forage for supplies. This certainty filled him with panic and resignation. The thought of going outside, alone, with three bullets in a gun that belonged in a museum, wearing women's tennis shoes because they were the only footwear he'd found that fitted his small feet, made him feel nauseous and weak.

The weather was worsening, rain and sleet and hailstones. A religious man might have seen it all as some kind of sign and prayed for divine providence, but George was beyond such acts and it comforted him in some strange way.

*

The next morning, George woke to silence and the fear he had fallen deaf during his sleep. There was no rain against the windows and walls. No sharp wind buffeting the house.

Gathering himself, he ate two stale digestive biscuits then went upstairs with a small helping of food for Royce.

He was thinking about the previous night's dreams and nightmares, when he opened the bedroom door and realised the room was empty.

*

George searched the house then went outside and paced upon the sodden grass and mud, but there was no sign of Royce. During the night, Royce had shifted the barricade from the front door, pulled back the bolts, and silently opened the door while George slept.

Panic worked inside him like busy hands while he concentrated to arrange the tumult of his thoughts. He wound his pocket watch and his eyes followed the moving clock hands.

THE LAST OUTPOST

Royce had left him alone. He was alone. He didn't want to be alone.

*

George left the house in the late morning, wrapped in several layers of clothing against the cold, the revolver in his hand. The hatchet was tucked into his belt. It was bitterly cold and the sky rained silent sleet. He adjusted the woollen hat and pulled up his hood, glancing around and looking over his shoulder for threats or movement. His stomach ached with hunger as the wind pulled at him. He folded his arms against his body, frail and worn, and grimaced at the sleet falling upon the mud and puddles of black water. The hills and fields were pitiless, bleak, exhausted by winter. The wind in the treetops sounded like the ocean.

Three fields on, where the land declined to the north and crumbling stone walls dripped rainwater, he found an infected man caught in the half-collapsed remains of a barbed wire fence.

George halted ten yards from the man, who stirred from a deep fugue and looked up at him. He was a pathetic thing, half-dead in the wire, deep cuts along his skin, most of them black and infected. Tufts of hair wilted on his scalp. His clothes were ripped to pieces. He reeked of algae-choked ponds and gangrene. The man's body had suffered terrible mutations in the soft parts of his body, and his stomach looked swollen. And for a moment George was fascinated and repulsed by the pulsing lesions on his back and the broken arrangement of his limbs. There was a faint hunger in the man's eyes, his sharp hands groped at the ground, and the wet wound of his mouth opened.

George stepped closer, careful not to slip on the mud, and crouched to be at eye level with the infected man.

"How long have you been here?" George glanced at the revolver. "Not fair, is it? This is how your life ends, trapped here, dying of hunger. I'll bet you once had dreams and hopes; a family, maybe. A job. Bills to pay. Mundane stuff." George noticed tattoos on the man's left arm, clouded by grime. He looked closer. Three names in simple lettering with cartoon hearts either side of them each. There was a birth date under each name.

"I was a father too," George said, and he swallowed a knot in his throat. Looked at the crescents of dirt under his fingernails. "Of course, they were already grown up by the time all this happened. I never found out what happened to them and their families. They had their own children. Suppose I'll never find out."

The man looked at the ground. A wet gust of breath from between his sore and cut mouth. George stood, put away the revolver and took out the hatchet.

The man's hand scraped on the ground a few yards from George's feet. He attempted to thrash in the wire, but the more he moved the deeper the barbs ripped into his skin and made him bleed. Then he became still, and the only sound was the crows in the far off trees.

George looked at the man, his voice soft and forgiving. "It's going to be okay."

*

The wind carried to him old smells of ash and charcoal from Starling House, even though it was not yet in sight past the trees. He moved through the small stretch of woodland, nervous and tired, the boughs dripping rainwater like the sounds of ticking clocks. The sleet rustled in the trees. When he broke through the treeline he saw the grass blackened with soot and heat. His trainers sunk into the waterlogged earth. The ruins of Starling House black against the tall trees beyond. The fire had torn through the house that night. Its heart had been burnt out. The walls were still intact but were scorched and frail. Human remains mouldered in the grass around the house; a ribcage curved upwards from a patch of thick weeds. A shattered spine and scattered segments of vertebrae like tossed stones. Rusted firearms beyond recovery. The small paw prints of scavengers.

George stood in what remained of the front doorway, pushed the blackened doors open and peered inside. Pools of shadow, holes in the floor, torn chasms. Fallen timber, black and crumbling.

Ragged scatterings of bricks and mortar. George tried not to look at the bones amidst the wrecked interior, but his eyes discerned every convex rib and angular jut of bone. The remaining floorboards were the colour of coal; he was reluctant to test his weight upon them.

"Royce?" His voice came back at him from the ruins. "Royce, are you here?" George glanced over his shoulder, fooled by the slipping of the wind through the grass that sounded like creeping feet sneaking up on him.

He looked at the blackened floor and winced. "Fuck." He put one foot forwards and felt the floor take its weight, exhaled and followed it with his other foot. He repeated this, avoiding the holes and broken bits, until he was standing in what had been the hallway. And he crept past jutting spikes of steel rebar, rubble and damp patches in the remaining walls where colonies of fungi glistened and flourished. Warped, twisted metal, ash and plaster. Charred doorways and crooked black corridors where pools of dirty water and glass like black slate reflected the grey light from the sky. A scorched, flayed corpse curled into itself upon the shambles of the floor.

George moved slowly, careful not to slip or trip, terrified at the prospect of the gutted house collapsing upon him.

He found Royce sitting and hunched over in the ruins, an ashen ghost among the wreckage. His clothes were damp and they smelled of it, and when

George approached, Royce raised his head and watched him and made no attempt to escape.

"I knew you'd be here," said George. Close up, George saw Royce's shoulders shaking, and his hands looked palsied and boneless as he clutched them to his stomach. His face was grey in the shadow of the burnt walls. He was crying, but there was no sound from his mouth.

"I couldn't find anything," Royce said.

"I know," said George. "Come on. Let's get out of here."

*

The wind had died, and with it the sleet and the rain. George and Royce were heading back to the farmhouse when Royce pointed out the plume of smoke rising from behind a copse of trees in a distant field. The men stopped. George watched the smoke disperse in the wind when it hit the sky.

"A campfire," Royce said. His face was sullen and the stains under his eyes were the colour of a bruised apple. His mouth moved awkwardly and he bit his lip. He looked at George.

"The men who chased us?" George said.

Royce shrugged and looked at the smoke, then turned away, and George followed him before his shivering form melted into the fields.

*

The dark came on like a veil thrown over the land. Royce was asleep in his room and George could tell by the things he muttered that in his dreams he was being chased. George placed a cup of water by the bedside and left the room, descending the stairs as the house moaned and creaked around him like an old schooner in a squall.

In the candlelight at the kitchen table he wound his pocket watch and tried to ignore the hunger clawing at the walls of his stomach. He put the watch down and stared at the table top. Ran a finger over ancient stains made in the long ago. Fracture-thin splits in the wood.

The scratching came again at the front door, and before he knew it he was standing by the door with the revolver in one hand and the other poised to open it. The scratching grew frenzied and he pictured those nails or claws gouging at the wood.

Why don't you come in?

He touched the doorknob and went to turn it, but the author of the scratching made a sound like pigs rutting and he lost his nerve against the squeals and shrieks and wet sounds. He backed away and pointed the gun at the door, worried about the thickness of the wood and how long it would take something with enthusiastic hands to burrow through it.

By the time the scratching went away and the terrible sounds stopped, George had retreated to the living room to huddle in a dark corner with the blankets piled about him.

CHAPTER TWENTY-TWO

In the morning, as the first light made a thin line of fire on the horizon, George went outside with the revolver to inspect the front of the house. He examined the scratch marks on the door and the darkening blood upon and around them. The grass around the front of the house had been trampled, but he couldn't discern any specific footprints.

He looked around at the countryside but there was no smoke, and when it started raining again he returned inside.

*

The day passed in a slow, dim trance of tiredness and hunger. A few mouthfuls of food were all he could take from the supplies. Royce slept for most of the day, and cried out in his dreams and nightmares.

George sat at an old mahogany desk and pored over hardback books of history and theology. There was quite a collection on the dusty shelves, filling an entire wall. The last owner of the house had been a devout bibliophile, it seemed. There were leather-bound editions from HP Lovecraft, William Hope Hodgson, Fritz Leiber, Clark Ashton Smith, Ambrose Bierce, MR James, and Robert W Chambers.

On the bottom shelf he found an old, creased paperback. A pulp western with a front cover that showed a grizzled gunslinger shooting a black-clad villain on a dirt street in some nameless frontier town.

He picked up the book, *Texan Blood Devils,* and flicked through the yellowed pages. The publication date inside the front cover was 1995.

He turned the book over and saw a photo of himself standing under the bough of some grey oak tree. A much younger George Carter, from another lifetime. Less grey hair. Staring through the looking glass. A time he could barely remember. He would have thought it a dream if it weren't for the photo.

George returned the paperback to its resting place among the dust and the other forgotten books.

He fell asleep at the desk, crumpling in his chair like a bag of broken sticks.

*

A hand on his shoulder woke George. He looked up at Royce with his mouth open and his heart kicking hard. The other man was like a shadow in the dancing candlelight. Whether it was because George had just woken, or the light in the study was failing due to the guttering flame, he couldn't make out Royce's face and for a moment he was terrified that Royce had become infected.

"There's something at the door," Royce said.

THE LAST OUTPOST

George had never been so glad to hear the man speak. Then he heard the scratching at the front door. He grabbed the revolver from the desk and followed Royce into the kitchen.

*

The thing behind the door grunted and wheezed, wet fingers scrabbling and raking. George and Royce stood several yards from the door and watched it tremble in its frame.

From the other side, the doorknob was turned as far as it could go, but the bolts and the lock kept it closed. George was breathing hard.

"We should kill it," said Royce, and there was nothing in his voice but dead words. He looked at George. There was a knife in his hand; George hadn't noticed it before.

"We should just wait for it to go away," said George. "It always goes away."

"It's too dangerous," said Royce. "It might attract others like it. We don't know what else is roaming around here. We could end up with a whole pack of infected outside the house."

Before George could think about it, Royce was at the door and pulling back the bolts.

"Stop it!" said George. "What are you doing?"

Royce grunted. "What we should have already done. You ready to use that poxy little pistol?" He turned the key in the lock, then twisted the handle and pulled the door back, stepping away with his knife raised. George saw something manic in Royce's face.

"Get ready, George!"

George looked towards the doorway and raised the revolver.

The door opened.

The naked creature was on all fours, hunched and bedraggled, with long stringy hair. The face peering through strands of black hair was like a porcelain mask, and when it opened its mouth to display rows of savage teeth George felt a little of something inside him dwindle and shrink away. It sniffed at the air and clawed at the linoleum floor, already halfway through the doorway. A sway of its head and a glimpse of pale, sightless eyes.

"Fucking bitch," Royce said.

The creature twitched at the sound of Royce's voice. Its white breasts sagged. Its bony limbs twitched. Torn and bloodied nails on its fingers. Blood dripping from between its legs like some terrible menstruation.

"Shoot it, George."

George hesitated, his finger on the trigger.

The creature screamed, salivating at the closeness of its prey. A rancid, moronic grin.

"Shoot the fucking thing!" Royce said.

George looked down the revolver's barrel. His insides were rising like fluid.

The creature raised its pallid face towards Royce.

It moved, feet scrabbling on the floor.

Royce shouted something.

Awful sounds and the stench of offal filled the kitchen.

As the gorge rose into his throat, George pulled the trigger.

CHAPTER TWENTY-THREE

They took the creature's body from the house and dumped it in a ditch half a mile away. They wore gloves and breathed cold air through face masks made of rags. Royce spoke about death as they stood at the edge of the ditch, looking down at the body.

"That boy I killed was in my dreams last," said Royce. "He called me a murderer."

"You're not a murderer," said George.

"Yes, I am. Not that it matters anymore. Murder is everywhere, George; all about us like smoke. I can smell it in the dirt and on our clothes. It's inevitable. It's the way of the world. Nature is murder, my friend." Royce kicked a clump of dirt into the ditch and it landed next to the woman's corpse. "How did you feel after killing her?"

"I felt terrible," George said. "Still do."

"But it had to be done. There was no choice."

George didn't reply.

Royce stared into the ditch. "Do you think we'll be punished for what we've done?"

George looked at him. "What do you mean?"

Royce exhaled, chewed on his lip then spat. "I don't know. I was from a Catholic family. Old stains never fade."

THE LAST OUTPOST

As they walked away, to return to the house, George looked back at where they'd left the woman's body and thought that if there were gods in the world they would take her soul with them before they fled this damp hell.

*

They were a hundred yards from the house when they saw the lone figure outside the front door. They crouched behind a hedgerow and peered through the weeds.

The figure was dressed in thick winter clothes, checking the windows for signs of occupancy. The person tried the door, but George had locked it before they left the house earlier.

"Who the fuck is that?" said Royce.

"A survivor," said George. He pulled down his mask.

"A scavenger." Royce had the knife in one hand. "Do you have the revolver on you?"

George looked at him. He felt for the weight of the gun in his pocket. "Yes."

"We have to protect what's ours," Royce said. "We can't let anyone take the house." He wiped at his mouth. "It looks like he doesn't have a gun, and we have the element of surprise.

"You want me to shoot him?" said George.

When Royce turned to him, his face was damp with sweat, his eyes were red-rimmed and bloodshot, and the way he showed his teeth when he opened his mouth turned George's stomach to soup. Dirt and grease in his beard and on the skin of his thin neck. "We have to defend the house from bad people."

George took the revolver from his pocket and Royce snatched it from his hand.

"What're you doing?"

"I'm protecting what is ours."

Royce began to stalk towards the house, and George whispered after him, but he ignored George and went on with the gun in his hand.

*

George watched helplessly as Royce crept up on the man. The low wind and the patter of the drizzle on the grass covered Royce's approach, and the man didn't turn until Royce was upon him. George was twenty yards behind, but as he approached Royce and the figure and the house beyond them, he slowed when he realised that the figure was a woman and underneath her winter clothes, her stomach was swollen and large.

Royce lowered the revolver and stared at the woman. George stood next to him. The woman, her face lined with exhaustion and her eyes livid, raised one hand in a greeting while the other rested upon her belly.

"Hello," she said, and she would have been beautiful if not for the end of the world.

THE LAST OUTPOST

*

The woman sat at the kitchen table with George sat across from her. Royce was standing with his arms folded in the doorway to the living room, watching the woman in the meek glow of the candlelight. It was nearly dark outside.

George offered her a glass of water, which she gulped down without pause. When she finished she put the glass down and looked at George, her lips damp and her body trembling beneath layers of cotton, polyester and wool. Her blonde hair was tied back in a loose knot. There were bits of twigs and dirt in her hair. She brushed away the strands of fringe that had fallen over her eyes. George couldn't imagine what she had seen and done to survive. His eyes kept flicking towards her belly: she had to sit back from the table because her stomach was too big for her to lean forward and rest her hands.

"Thank you," she said in a soft West Country lilt to her voice. "You're the first people I've seen in almost two weeks. Uninfected people, that is."

"I don't think there're many of us left," George said.

She put her hands on her stomach. "I hope you're wrong."

"Me too."

"My name's Amy."

"I'm George. That's Royce. Are you hungry?"

"Yes."

George gave her a tin of spaghetti and meatballs. She peeled the tin open and spooned the food with her hands into her mouth.

"It's not much," George said. "But it's all we can spare." He watched her eat. She was ravenous. Such desperate hunger scared him a little.

Amy finished the food and placed the tin on the table. "Thanks, anyway."

"Where are you from, Amy?"

"Tiverton," she said.

"I'm from Exeter," George said. "Tiverton's not far from there."

"I used to go shopping with my mum in Exeter." Something in her face slackened, like she was recalling a particular memory. "It was nice."

"What happened to you?" Royce asked. George glanced at him and frowned.

"Same as everyone else," Amy said. "The plague. The outbreak. Bad news for everyone."

"How did you end up here?" George said.

"I was with a group of people." She paused and glanced at the floor. "I don't need to tell you what happened to the rest of them. Now it's just me. Well, me and the bump."

"Is the father…?"

"My husband. Dead." No emotion in her voice. "He was killed by a pack of infected near Yeovil." She looked down at her stomach. "We didn't get a chance to find out if it's a boy or a girl. But I think it's a girl."

"A girl?" Royce said. "You sure?"

Amy nodded and her mouth held the thinnest curve of a smile.

"How far gone are you?" said George.

"About six months," she said.

George fidgeted with his hands on the table. "It must be difficult."

"Don't feel bad for me," Amy said. "She's all that's kept me going. If I wasn't for her, I would have given up long ago."

"Where are you heading?" said George.

After sipping at a bottle of water from her pack, she wiped her mouth with her thin hands and cleared her throat. "I'm going to the east coast."

George frowned. "Why the east coast? What's there?"

"I'd heard there's a survivors' outpost in Denmark. I'm hoping to find a boat and travel across the North Sea."

"Denmark? Fucking hell. Sounds like a suicide mission," said Royce.

"Where did you hear about this outpost?" George said.

"My husband and I were told about it at one of the refugee camps. Other people were going to make the journey too. The remnants of the British military are there, according to what we heard."

"So it was just a rumour," said Royce.

Amy shook her head. "More than a rumour. Radio broadcasts."

"Even if there was an outpost in Denmark, it might have been destroyed already," Royce said. "I never heard anything about it. And you'd have to survive crossing the North Sea first. Do you realise how difficult that will be?"

"The outpost is still there. And I can look after myself."

"How do you know it's still there?" George said.

"I'll show you."

CHAPTER TWENTY-FOUR

Amy took a wind-up radio from within her pack and set it on the table. It was about the size of a brick, scratched and dirty from its travels.

"We're just in time," she said as she checked her watch.

Royce stepped over to the table and took a chair. He looked at George. Amy flicked a switch on the radio's side. George felt a tingle of anticipation in his stomach as he drew closer to the radio. The crackle and whisper of static, the sound of the atmosphere and solar winds.

Amy moved the radio to the other side of the table: a voice began to emerge through the distortion and interference. George listened. Royce leaned forward, his face creasing in the candlelight, the shadows under his eyes like smudges of coal.

A man's voice, barely audible.

"Right on time," Amy said. She twisted the dial and the voice became clearer and louder. George stared at the radio with his mouth open.

"...survivors...from the infected...we are in Denmark. 55° 28' 0" North, 8° 27' 0" East. A seaport town called Esbjerg. A community of survivors. We offer protection and safety. We are fighting back against the plague. There is hope here. All is not lost. I repeat: all is not lost..."

The message was repeated in Danish, Norwegian, French and German before the transmission ended, and when Amy turned off the radio the silence it left behind weighed heavily like the aftermath of an accusation. Royce wiped at his face. George put one hand to his mouth. Amy looked at the men, her dirty face hopeful and pale.

"I can't believe it," said George.

"They repeat the message on the hour, every hour," said Amy. "Different people, different nationalities. They take it in turn, like a rota system."

"Do you think it's real?" said Royce. "It might be a trap, a way to lure people there."

"For what reason?" Amy said.

"Humans are capable of horrendous things," said Royce. "Particularly now."

"We ran into some people a few weeks ago," said George. "It didn't end well."

"You'd ignore it, then?" Amy asked.

"I didn't say that."

"It's hope," said Amy. "Hope for my baby. Hope for all of us."

Royce didn't seem impressed. "Hope is a fickle bitch."

*

The dark came on and pressed against the windows. They shared the last tin of baked beans and talked about the old world. Movies and songs, celebrities and TV shows. Amy talked about her favourite albums and George lamented the loss of freshly-baked bread and cream cakes. Royce didn't say much, just drank from the old bottle of gin he'd found in the cupboard under the stairs and grew steadily more drunk as the night passed. They did not talk about their lost loved ones.

At some point in the night they heard a high-pitched shriek from somewhere out in the fields; it silenced them and prompted George to keep the revolver by his side.

Amy slept on the sofa, swamped in blankets, while Royce retired to his bedroom with what remained of the gin to leave George alone with his thoughts, his fears, and his hunger scraping at his guts. He sat at the kitchen table, listening to the hourly broadcasts from Denmark. Between the transmissions he used a bread knife to carve the names of dead people into the table.

He kept the volume low and leaned his face close to the radio, wishing he could reply to them; to plead with them to save him, Royce, Amy, and her unborn baby.

He sat there for a long time.

The voices of all the people brought him to tears.

*

Amy was already up and gathering her belongings when George woke. He remembered his dreams of maternity wards being ravaged by the infected.

"Morning," said Amy. She sipped water from a bottle.

George stood. "Morning." He looked around. "I guess Royce isn't up yet."

"What happened to him?" Amy said.

"Last night?"

"Before. During the outbreak."

"Oh, right. He had a family. A daughter. But he can't remember what they looked like because he lost all the things he had to remember them."

Amy nodded, stroked her stomach.

George looked at the names carved in the table.

"Will you and Royce come with me?" Amy said. "To the coast, at least. I could use the company, and there's safety in numbers, don't you think?"

"I thought about it last night," George said. He looked around the cold grey kitchen and thought that if he stayed here for another night it would be the end of him. "There's nothing here. We've almost run out of food."

"So is that a 'yes'?"

"Do you trust us?" he said.

"As much as I need to. I don't have a choice. If you or Royce were going to rape or kill me, you'd have done it by now."

"It's a long way to go. Somerset to the east coast. We'll have to walk if we can't find a vehicle. Chances are we won't make it. And even if we do, there's still the North Sea to be crossed."

"I have to try," said Amy. "What else is there to do?"

Royce appeared in the doorway; they hadn't heard him descend the stairs. He rubbed his eyes, the smell of stale gin and vomit steaming off him. "Are we leaving?"

"If you want to, Royce," Amy said. "We'll go together."

His eyes lingered on her stomach. He sighed. "Fair enough. Better to die out there than in this shithole."

He turned away and returned upstairs.

*

They listened to the next broadcast and gathered their remaining provisions. There was hardly any food and only two bottles of water between them. George was dismayed when he remembered there were only two bullets left in the revolver and there was such a long way to go. He thought he would die on the road with Amy and Royce. But it was better to die in the rain with the sky above you than inside a stinking house full of other people's memories.

"Maybe we should burn the house down," said Royce.

"Let's just go," said George.

Amy nodded biting her lip.

"Are you okay?" George asked her.

"I'll be fine once we get going," she said. She saw Royce watching her, but said nothing.

"We'll need to find a vehicle eventually," George said. "Otherwise it'll take weeks to walk to the coast, and I don't think we're capable of that."

Royce looked out the window. "It's raining. What a surprise."

They went out into the rain and left the house behind. George turned back one last time and was glad to leave.

CHAPTER TWENTY-FIVE

They were hungry when they left the house and the drizzle was constant upon them. Three grey, slumped shapes meandering across the countryside. Bowed heads and shuffling footsteps. George imagined the land all ransacked and devastated, the three of them as transients walking the hills. He turned his head to appraise the land around them, and wondered if leaving the house was a grave mistake and it would kill them.

"An aberration of a world," Royce said to the ground, his hands close to his face. George looked at him, but Royce stared straight ahead, down the road where it stretched into the rain. George didn't ask what he'd meant. He watched Amy scuffing her feet beside them, her face peering out from beneath her dripping hood. She coughed, wiped her mouth, and exhaled white mist into the air as she clutched her coat to her body like she was scared of losing it. The coat's hem flapped around her knees.

George put one hand to his stomach and felt the prominent ribs under his clothes. His throat was raw and dry, so he raised his face to the sky and opened his mouth to catch the rain.

*

With his foot Royce poked the carcass of a deer half-hidden in the nettles at the side of the road. The deer had been dead for a while, the skin and flesh stripped away along its spine. Yellowed bones and wet fur. A flayed hide under the rain. Its eyes were gone.

"I wonder what killed it," said Amy. She looked around. "Infected?"

"Doesn't matter," said George. "It's been dead a long time. Whatever killed it is probably long gone."

"I hope you're right."

"I rarely am."

*

The peak of a church tower and a wind-blown flag atop it rose above the ranks of distant trees.

There was a car on the road. Royce searched its boot while George checked the compartment under the dashboard and Amy sat in the driver's seat and rested her legs. She drank from her water bottle and when she saw how much was left she slumped back against the seat. George found nothing of use in the front of the car. A user's manual and a paperback novel with a bookmark near the end. Royce appeared from behind the car and shook his head when George asked if he'd found anything.

They rested for a while, sheltering from the rain, listening to the tapping of the downpour on the roof. George suggested trying the village for supplies. Amy tried the ignition, but the car was dead and the scraping of something in the broken engine was its death-rattle.

They waited until the rain stopped before they moved on.

*

The first house they came to had been burnt from within and the glass was gone from the windows. George checked the ruins but there was only ash inside the walls.

They found the first scarecrow soon afterwards, strapped into a cruciform shape upon a wooden cross and planted in an overgrown garden, limbs of rotting straw jutting from the moth-eaten suit jacket covering its raggedy torso. A bowler hat upon its cloth-covered head, atop a face with a merry smile painted in red. The eyeholes had been pecked out by birds. Spikes of the rank straw spilling through the knees of its tattered corduroy trousers. Royce stared at the blind effigy until George placed one hand on his shoulder, and he turned to look at George and his face was wan and bewildered.

"Come on," George said, worried about the look in Royce's eyes.

Royce nodded. Amy was standing behind them, looking down the road into the village.

"There are more," she said.

Other lawns held scarecrows clothed in jumble sale rags and assorted ludicrous hats. One of them wore a woman's summer hat similar to one George's mother used to wear when he was a boy and the family went on trips to the seaside.

They searched the nearby houses for food, but found nothing. George felt like crying but he was too tired.

"Stripped clean," said Royce, chewing on a fingernail.

Amy looked at the men and dug her hands inside her pockets, shivering in the cold. The drizzle was falling again, slowly turning to sleet.

"Are you okay?" George asked her.

She nodded and tried to smile. "Fine. Just hungry."

"We'll find something," said George.

"I wouldn't bet on it," Royce said.

"There has to be something left to eat."

Royce said nothing, just stared at the scarecrows as if he was waiting for them to animate and come shuffling towards him on their legs of mouldering straw.

*

There was a man crucified on the village green, and by the deterioration of the corpse he had been there for weeks. Putrid and sunken, skin almost black with rot. A stench of corruption. His eyes were gone, pecked away by birds, like the scarecrow's. Scavengers had been at the soft parts of the body where the stained clothes were torn. His hands had been nailed to the horizontal wooden beam, palms facing outwards, and there were long, thick iron spikes through his ankles, which had also been lashed to the vertical beam. A cord of rotting rope around his neck kept him tightened to the wooden cross.

"Oh my god," said Amy. She laid her hands on her stomach in a protective gesture. "Why would someone do that to a person?"

"Madness," said Royce. "Peel away the skin of Man..."

"I wonder who he was," said Amy. "What did he do to deserve this?"

No one answered.

"Should we cut him down?"

George and Royce exchanged a look; Royce shrugged and looked away.

"There's nothing we can do for him," George said, staring at the body. "His suffering is over."

*

In one of the houses on the next street, they scrounged a tin of marrowfat peas fallen down the back of a kitchen cupboard and missed by other scavengers. George checked that the tin was intact before he pocketed it.

Night closed in and the shrill calls of the infected came out of the growing dark. George and Royce secured the house as best they could and settled with Amy in the living room and shared the peas in the shivering flame of a candle. George sat in the dust-stinking armchair and with his thumb and forefinger picked cold peas from the small amount in his other hand, placing them in his mouth and cringing as his teeth mashed them into paste. When he looked at Royce and Amy they wore similar expressions. Royce sat on the floor with his back against the section of wall by the bay window. Amy slumped on the sofa, dirty blankets over her shoulders and legs. George finished his portion and licked the pea-juice from his hands, while Amy drank the water left in the tin. Nothing was left to waste.

*

And then they talked of the old things and customs now obsolete in the plague-ravaged world.

"I miss Facebook," Amy said, the faintest hint of a smile on her face. "My husband told me I was addicted to it. I loved playing Candy Crush."

"What's Candy Crush?" said George.

"It's a game," Royce said.

George frowned. "Sounds like a waste of time."

"It was," Royce said. "I preferred FarmVille."

Amy wiped at one eye. "I wish I had given my husband more attention instead of playing stupid games on the computer. But you never think it'll come to an end, do you? You think things will always carry on the way they are and you'll have plenty of time to sort things out." She looked at the candle's flame, her mouth thin, eyes aglow and glassy. "He was a good man, and he always did the right thing. He didn't deserve to die."

"We've all got regrets," said George. "I wish I could have said goodbye to my son and his family. My grandsons." He closed his eyes and saw Billy and Daniel, but it was just a glimpse of them and they were soon gone, back into the dark. "I don't even know if they're alive or dead. Part of me thinks it'd be better if they were dead, then I could mourn for them." His windpipe tightened and something hard formed in his throat.

Royce was watching George. The house breathed around them. The night, at least in this little corner of the world, seemed peaceful, and George was grateful for that.

Royce cleared his throat and he looked at the floor between his feet. "I'd give anything to see my wife and daughter again. I'd kill to see them again. Just for that one last chance."

Then Royce was silent, and soon they were all asleep.

*

George awoke in the night to the sound of titans in the sky, high above the house. He pulled the blanket up to his chest and listened, fascinated and terrified.

What are you? Where are you from?

Eventually the titans moved away. Amy was sobbing quietly within the darkness. He listened to her, ashamed to be doing so, as if he were a voyeur to her grief. He thought about her unborn child and imagined it as something alien and writhing ripping itself from Amy's womb when the time had come for it to be born. He imagined, with a shiver of revulsion, a plague-ridden thing that would feed on its mother for sustenance, and kill her by doing so.

It took him a long while to get back to sleep.

CHAPTER TWENTY-SIX

George was awake before first light. From an upstairs window he watched the first stains of yellow, orange and red on the horizon. The sky was clear except for some distant banks of cloud, and he hoped it was a good sign. He was light-headed and thirsty, like a man made of dried sticks and dust. He rested against a wall and ran his hands over his face, his teeth itching and aching, and moaned at the discomfort of his grinding bones. He looked into the mirror on the landing and dread filled him at the thought of the day ahead. If they couldn't find a working vehicle with fuel, they'd be forced to walk, and he knew deep down he wasn't capable of it. And he would die on the road.

He walked downstairs and found Royce standing by the living room window, peering through a gap in the curtains as Amy slept. Royce turned his head towards George and put his forefinger across his mouth. He flicked his head towards the window. His knife was in his hand.

George went to the edge of the window and pulled the curtains back just enough so he could see outside through the net curtain. He flinched at the sight of infected people moving past the house and down the road, heading back the way he, Royce and Amy had travelled. They filled the street from one side of the road to the other, trampling over gardens and lawns. George attempted to count their number, but he couldn't keep up with the flow of bodies marching past. There were hundreds. A swarm. George watched them pass in their droves – malformed limbs and mouths; weeping sores and thin tendrils erupting from skin. Appalling effigies of men, women and children. Naked bodies entangled into hellish shapes. Faces stripped of skin, sprouting cilia and glistening stingers. Shambling figures screamed at the sky. Hairless things with onyx claws, pale spikes rising from their spines. Some of them still wore the remnants of their clothes, torn and flapping and filthy with bloodstains and dried excrement. There were soldiers among them, those who had succumbed to the plague during the battle for the mainland. People from all walks of life, classes and professions, all of them joined in their hunger to infect and feed. Driven by the terrible pestilence.

A priest stumbled past, still wearing his dog collar and black garments, his twisted ankle trailing behind him. The mandibles of his jaws were distended and twinging, his face covered in lesions, and something pink and worm-like darted from his dripping mouth. Many of the infected bore injuries and wounds. Gangrenous limbs all thin and inflamed, shivering in the cold air. The stench of their unwashed bodies and infected sores must have been horrendous.

Royce said nothing as he watched them. Neither did George; he was filled with awe and horror. Words were scant things against such a sight.

Gradually the swarm dwindled into wandering packs and lone stragglers and then they were gone. George moved away from the window and sat down to calm the shaking of his limbs, the riot of his heart.

*

After searching several houses already looted bare, they left the village by way of the main road, exhausted and hungry under a clear sky. But the sun was weak and did nothing to warm them. There had been nothing for breakfast but a few sips of water each. George wanted to sleep, wanted the world to go away. He looked at Amy and saw her rubbing her stomach.

"Is everything okay, Amy?"

When she raised her face to him, her eyes were reddened and a cold sore wept at the corner of her mouth. The look in her eyes forced George to turn away and watch the road ahead of them.

They picked through the remains of car wrecks, checking compartments and down the backs of seats. George found a small teddy bear and gave it to Amy for her unborn child. She nodded her thanks and stared at it for a while in her hand before she packed it away.

Royce was watching them. "There's nothing here." He spat by his feet then looked at the sky. He appeared near-skeletal in the sunlight.

They walked on.

*

Several days passed, spent evading swarms of infected and toiling through silent villages. George had drunk some river water and spent most of one day shitting in hedgerows. There was barely anything to eat and Amy drunk the final dregs of water in the last bottle. They were starving, dragged down by thirst, peeling away their resolve and what remained of their strength.

Amy cried when she realised her baby had stopped kicking.

Days faded into nothing. Consumed by dreams of water and food. Nightmares of the infected. Monsters in the fields. George drank his own tears. Time became meaningless. Night and day and screams in the dark. Huddling together in the tombs of houses.

It began to snow, and soon the ground was covered.

They walked the roads until Amy stopped and could go no further. She cried into her hands as she slumped by the roadside. George and Royce went to her, sheltering her from the falling snow with blankets pulled from their packs. Their shivering forms and chattering teeth. No one spoke. George was too tired to open his mouth, and he could feel his limbs growing numb and his heart slowing. His eyelids were heavy, and it was a struggle to keep his eyes open. His head nodding. Snow drifting against his face. The wail of the wind down the road.

He thought about the child inside Amy, wondered if it were better this way, instead of being born into misery, starvation and violence. Her baby would feel no pain and suffering, no hunger and sadness. No madness. No knowledge of the world and the black ruins of everything. There would be no fading of the light, and then that would be the end.

CHAPTER TWENTY-SEVEN

There is nothing but flesh. It feeds and assimilates, bringing communion to millions. Mouths, limbs and claws, tentacles, tusks and eyes. Always feeding, always infecting. Minds and memories consumed. The plague is elegant in its design, and without fear. It is all-consuming and has no conception of mercy and compassion. No love, no hate, nothing. When there is nothing left to sustain it, the plague will gestate and begin its next stage of evolution.

But for now, it feeds.

*

Royce woke on a hard floor with blankets wrapped around him and a pillow under the back of his head. His first breath was a desperate gasp for air. His limbs like stone and his lungs were flapping sacks. He looked at the dusty light casing on the ceiling, his eyes stinging, and put one hand to his head to quell the pounding at the centre of his skull. The lethargic, painful movement of his mouth made him think his lips had been stitched together and then pulled apart at some point while he was passed out. When he tried to rise from his back, a thin hand was placed on his shoulder.

"Easy," an old voice said. "It's alright."

THE LAST OUTPOST

The sensation of movement underneath him. The grinding of a large engine and wheels over an uneven road. The scrape of an axle, a jarring suspension, and metal rattling in a composite of parts. He was aware of shapes around him, and the smell of unwashed skin and hair, and old breath. Bacteria on teeth. The musk of dried sweat and garments that had clothed bodies for weeks at a time. The fetid, pungent smell of bodies in an enclosed space.

"It's alright," the voice said again in a soft Scottish accent.

He didn't trust the voice and tried again to rise, but other hands pressed gently on his shoulders and pushed him down. His vision swayed. The hands were all bony and he thought the fingers upon them were long-nailed, and when he looked at one of the hands placed near his neck he was sure it resembled a pale spider twitching in proximity to his open mouth.

An old woman was sitting by his side, leaning over him. She poked at his face with one gnarled finger, and the thought of that finger slipping into his mouth made him shiver. She was wizened and narrow, all sharp angles, the slit of her mouth working between the frayed strands of long grey hair. There were other faces, too, but he couldn't focus on them.

"Where am I?"

"You're safe," she said.

Two of those who had gathered around him moved away, and he looked to his left and saw

George lying on his back in a wrapping of blankets, eyes closed, face deathly pale.

"George…" Royce muttered.

"He's fine," the woman said. "So is the young lady you were with. Don't worry. You're safe here." Her eyes were like glass stained deep blue, and he found them both comforting and slightly disconcerting.

Royce looked over the woman's shoulder, at the darkness past the windows.

*

It was daylight when he next woke and rose on to his elbows and looked around. The vehicle had stopped. Sweat on his brow and the vague sense of a fever inside him. George was gone, as were the other people, but Royce wasn't alone. The woman who had comforted him last night was crouching in a corner, reading a tattered Shaun Hutson paperback, her blue eyes following the lines of prose until she looked up at him over the top of the page and smiled. She lowered the book and placed it on the floor among heaps of blankets, bags and cardboard boxes. Royce noticed the handle of a knife tucked into the belt of her loose trousers. Coiled scarves surrounded her neck above a woollen jumper and a thick fleece coat. Her fingers were decorated with tarnished rings.

"Take it easy, Royce," she said. "Don't want you keeling over."

"How do you know my name?"

"George told us."

"Oh."

"I'm Sister Fiona."

"You're a nun?"

"Not exactly."

She crouched down next to Royce and offered him a plastic cup of water. She smelled of damp grass. Royce looked at the cup then her harshly-lined face.

"It's not poisoned, if that's what you're thinking," she said. "We're not murderers. Get it down you."

Royce's throat was raw. "Is this real? Is this a dream?"

Sister Fiona shook her head. "No dream. I'm as real as you are."

He swallowed, licked his lips, and the coolness of the cup in his hand tempted him to the water. And before he'd given it any more thought he was gulping at the water and he didn't stop until the cup was empty. He put down the cup and breathed hard, droplets on his beard.

Royce looked underneath the blankets. He was wearing different clothes.

"We had to change your clothes," Sister Fiona said. "They were ruined. Luckily we've got spares." Hooking her arms around him, she helped him up from the floor. She was stronger than her thin body suggested. Once Royce was on his feet, she let go of him, and he pulled the blanket tight around his shoulders. The thought of food birthed a moan at the base of his throat. The floor seemed to be moving, even though the vehicle was stationary. He wavered, but she steadied him. Her fingers dug into his clothes and against his skin. He noticed his boots were to one side, stuck between two bin bags bulging with children's clothes.

"Where's George and Amy?" he said. He was prepared for bad news.

"They're on the other coach," she said.

Royce looked at his surroundings. The moisture on the insides of the windows hid the world outside. The last four rows of seats had been removed to create an open area to store provisions and equipment. He stared down the aisle between the empty moquette seats. Overhead compartments were crammed with plastic bags of food and water.

"Where are we?" Royce asked.

Sister Fiona smiled thinly, deepening the creases in her face. "Let's go outside."

*

Royce descended the steps to the wet ground. Sister Fiona followed in her clunking boots and stood to one side of him, her hands hidden in the front folds of her coat. The ground was patchy with thawing snow and the air was cold enough to bite at his face with blunt teeth. He looked back at the coach he'd woken within; another coach was parked behind, where two men in oil-grimed clothes were tinkering with the engine at the front of the vehicle. The sides of both coaches were dented and scratched, covered in dried blood. The blood of the infected.

"The other coach broke down," Sister Fiona said.

There were people out in the field, next to the road where the two coaches were parked. A breath caught in Royce's throat as he stared at a gathering of about a dozen children dressed in winter clothes who giggled and whooped as they threw snowballs at one another. Woollen hats with bobbles covered their heads and scarves trailed from their necks. The sound of them, their laughter and chatter, nearly brought tears to his eyes.

Sister Fiona watched him watch the children.

"I haven't seen any children in months," Royce said. "I thought they were all dead or infected.

Beyond the children, further into the field, small groups of men carried shotguns, axes or bludgeons; watching the perimeter. There was a lookout with binoculars on the roof of each coach. Two women keeping an eye on the children glanced at Royce and talked with their faces close to one another.

Some people were on their knees, praying in the snow.

"Who are you people?" Royce said to Sister Fiona.

She smiled and looked at the children. "We're people of faith, Royce. We're survivors. Just like you and your friends."

"I'm not a man of faith," he said.

"That doesn't matter," she said. "We all have to walk our own path."

Several dozen crows lifted from the trees at the far end of the field. The men turned that way, ready for whatever had disturbed them to come out of the trees, but nothing emerged and the crows flew away.

"Ah, one of our new arrivals," a voice said behind them.

Royce turned. A thin, bald man with a scarred face and pale eyes had appeared next to Sister Fiona. He was no taller than the woman. The scar ran from under his left eye and down to his prominent chin. He wore a stained coat and muddy boots. Several layers of clothing added bulk to his form.

"Hello, Royce. I'm glad to see that you're up and about." His accent was straight out of the Home Counties. Royce shook the man's offered hand and tried not show his discomfort at the leathery fingers on his skin.

"Hello," Royce said.

The man smiled, but it seemed strained and not entirely honest. "I'm Marek. Pleased to meet you. We haven't seen many other survivors lately."

"Marek is our leader," Sister Fiona said. She wiped her mouth.

"I dislike that term," Marek said. "I'm more of a father figure to our people. *Leader* sounds so authoritarian, don't you think?"

Sister Fiona nodded and looked to the ground, as if chastised.

"I suppose so," Royce muttered.

"How are you feeling?" Marek didn't break eye contact.

"Bit of a headache. Nothing severe."

"We found you and your friends by the side of the road, huddled together and half-frozen. Another hour out there and you'd have been dead. You were lucky we found you; we were only on that road because we'd been turned back another way by a fallen tree."

"Lucky, I guess," Royce said.

Marek smiled. The corner of one eye twitched. "I think we were supposed to find you, Royce. Luck had nothing to do with it."

CHAPTER TWENTY-EIGHT

There were more people on the broken-down coach, sat in the seats, standing in the aisle or at the back of the vehicle. Marek muttered greetings to his people and left Royce to make his own way. Faces regarded Royce, nodding at him; most of them were pale and docile, some appeared maudlin. The smell of body odour everywhere. Furtive glances and muted greetings from mouths reluctant to open. Many of the seated people wore baseball caps and woollen hats, like apocalyptic tourists. A young woman with pretty eyes smiled warmly at Royce, and it was such an unexpected gesture that he could only stare blankly at her as he passed.

He imagined how he appeared to them, an ashen ghoul shambling out of the wastelands. A scarecrow man wandering in from the cold.

The back of the coach had been modified much the same as the other coach. The back rows of seats had been removed and piles of supplies lined the edges of the open area. Royce followed the smell of soup or stew to the far end of the coach, where people were gathered around a steaming pot on a portable stove. He winced at the hunger cramps and held his stomach.

George called to Royce and rose from the floor where he'd been sitting and limped towards him. There was a moment of uncertainty between the men. No handshake or awkward hug. A small smile on George's face.

"How are you feeling?" George asked. He looked hungry and tired, withered inside his clothes.

"As well as can be," Royce said. "Knackered."

George rubbed one eye with his knuckles. "Same here."

"I was ready to die," said Royce. "I'd accepted it."

"I was actually relieved," George said. "And then we get another chance. Strange how things work out, isn't it?"

Royce exhaled. "Where's Amy?"

George pointed to a sleeping form huddled within a mound of blankets. "She's fine." He fiddled with his hands and looked around, then looked back to Royce. "We don't know about the baby yet."

Royce said nothing while he looked at Amy, and in the stillness of her sleeping face there was no difference between sleep and death.

*

After Royce and George ate bowls of soup and drank cups of water offered to them by kindly women, they went outside with Marek. The sky had clouded over and threatened rain. Royce raised his collar against the wind coming off the low hills. George rubbed his hands together then folded his arms.

They stopped and watched an old woman lead the children into prayer.

"You're probably wondering who we are," said Marek.

Royce and George exchanged an unsure glance.

"We're just grateful that you helped us," said George.

"Who are you?" Royce asked Marek, before George could continue.

Marek placed his hands together. "We are the Family." He looked at them in turn, as if the name should have meant something.

Royce had a bad feeling, and it wasn't indigestion from guzzling down the soup. "What is that exactly?"

"We are a gathering of believers. Like-minded people."

"Believers in what?" said Royce. "Sister Fiona said you're people of faith."

Marek smiled, meek and warm and humble. "Believers in Almighty God, of course."

"You're a cult," said Royce.

"Pardon me?"

"A cult."

George made a disapproving sound.

Marek smiled again, but something in his eyes had changed, and he showed too many teeth for Royce's liking. "No, we're not a cult. Not at all. I think you're mistaken, Royce. We've been preparing for the End

Times; readying ourselves for the apocalypse, so when we win the final battle we can start again, throw away the old problems and prejudices that have forever plagued Mankind. A clean slate, if you will. We welcome anyone to join us."

Royce nodded at the armed men in the field. "You've got plenty of weapons."

"A necessary evil," said Marek. "We wouldn't have survived without them. We number forty-six souls, not including Amy and both of you. Five families among us. We have lost a few brothers and sisters along the way, of course."

"You've been on the road since the outbreak started?"

"No. We had lived in a commune near Exmoor, since the forming of the Family over forty years ago. Our ancestral home, you might call it. We held out against the infected for a while, and then they finally breached our walls two days ago. Luckily we were ready to evacuate, so our losses were minimal, but we knew we could never return to our home. We had to leave to survive."

Royce said, "Where are you heading?"

"The east coast, like you. And then across the North Sea."

"The Danish outpost."

"We had a long-wave radio," said Marek. "We picked up the first transmission two weeks ago. Unfortunately the radio was left behind when we abandoned the commune. Once the infected got inside, there wasn't time to save it."

"So you'll all be taking a ship across to Denmark?"

Marek nodded, pleased with himself. "One of our men used to pilot a fishing vessel, so operating another boat shouldn't be a problem."

"If you can find anything to use," said Royce.

"I'm sure we'll find something," Marek said. "If not, we'll find another way."

Royce looked at George. The old man shrugged, shivering against the deepening cold.

Marek was staring into the distance, and when he spoke, his voice was faint, as if his mind were somewhere else. "God will not fail us." He turned back towards them. "If you'll excuse me, I have to check on our mechanics, see how the repairs are going." Voice louder.

They watched Marek walk away.

"I don't trust him," said Royce.

George looked at the praying children. "They've got food, water and supplies. And weapons. Don't forget they saved our lives, Royce. Amy needs help with the baby – and neither of us is qualified for that. We're not even capable."

"The baby could already be dead," said Royce. "And the Danes could have been massacred by now."

"We have to try," said George.

"Why do you want to survive?" Royce asked him.

"To help Amy and the baby."

"What if the baby's dead?"

"Then I'll survive for those children over there," George said. "They're the future."

"The future is pretty fucked, George."

The old man didn't reply.

Royce folded his arms and rubbed them to rekindle some warmth in his skin. "Do you still have the pistol?"

George shook his head. "They took it from me when I was passed out. The hatchet, too."

"They took my knife," Royce said.

"Marek said he's looking after them, for our own safety."

"Fuck's sake." Royce shook his head and watched the children praying in the cold.

CHAPTER TWENTY-NINE

An hour later, Marek announced that the engine was fixed and the Family would be on the move again. There were cheers, and arms were raised in half-hearted celebration, while others clapped and thanked their god. Royce watched them all and said nothing.

Soon afterwards they were on the road and heading east. Royce sat next to George and looked out the window at the sleet falling over the withered land. Sister Fiona was taking care of Amy at the rear of the bus; she had woken earlier and talked to Royce and George, had laid her hands on her stomach, and the loss and pain in her eyes was such that Royce would have given his own life to guarantee the life of the unborn child. He would have given himself freely to whichever god demanded a sacrifice. A life for a life.

But there was nothing he or George or any of the others could do for her but wait.

He felt drowsy, the vehicle's motion making his eyelids heavy. The heaters on the coach were on full-blast. He fell asleep to the sound of children muttering old rhymes, and his last thought before darkness took him was his grievance with the heart-breaking fate of all life, to age and falter and die.

THE LAST OUTPOST

*

Royce dreamed about the first days of the outbreak. The monsters scratching at the windows of his home while his wife tried to calm their baby daughter crying upstairs. The burning houses and the burning streets; the infected stalking through the smoke. He remembered seeing the little girl from next door – she had just celebrated her tenth birthday – standing in the middle of the road with blood down the front of her pyjamas, jerking her head from side-to-side like a predator catching the scent of prey downwind. He had only looked once at her face before he turned away.

Another dream: he was sitting in his seat on the coach, and the vehicle had stopped in the road. The seats were occupied, but the people seated ahead of him would not turn to show him their faces. And he was too scared to look at the people behind him, because he was terrified of the wet rattling of their breathing and the low growls from their mouths.

*

George was asleep. Royce watched the countryside move past. Roving packs of infected in the fields. He saw two bloodstained women chase an injured deer from a dense thicket and bring it down upon the ground. The poor animal struggled as the infected set to it with their hands, teeth and squirming things that emerged from epidermal rents.

A thought came to him, fleeting but undeniable; a worm burrowing into the soft meat of his mind.

They will wipe this world clean.

The infected screamed at the coach as it passed.

*

Royce awoke, dull and listless, sunken in the seat, his limbs aching at the grind of the coach's wheels on the rutted roads. The smell of damp clothes around him made him feel sick.

"You were talking in your sleep," said George.

"Oh. Sorry."

"I was glad for the conversation."

"Thank you, George."

"For what?"

"Taking care of me after what happened at Starling House."

George hesitated. "Don't mention it."

"How have we survived?" Royce looked at the old man.

"Luck, I suppose," George said.

"But luck runs out eventually."

"Yes."

"Do you think we'll survive long enough to see Denmark?"

"I didn't think you were that bothered," George said.

"It's just a question."
"Go back to sleep, Royce."

*

The coaches resorted to back roads when they found the main thoroughfares blocked by car wrecks and debris. One road had been thick with the wrecks of over thirty cars and an artic lorry lying on its side across both lanes. Sometimes there were bones on the grass verges. Sometimes the infected skittered from the undergrowth with black claws raised to their chests. Royce saw a human torso amongst the thin branches of a tree, like something stored for later consumption.

It was slow going on the roads made treacherous by snow, mud, ice and rainwater. The coaches negotiated flooded roads and fallen trees. Men had to disembark and push car wrecks to the sides of the road so the coaches could pass.

Royce studied the members of the Family around him. They treated Royce and George with the sort of benign disdain reserved for stray dogs. The Family was an insulated community of believers. They were a herd. They were sheep, told what to do by Marek.

Royce wondered how many religions had survived the plague. Islam, Christianity, Judaism, Hinduism, Sikhism. All those different sects of Christianity. Scientology. Were they mostly gone, wiped away, their members either dead or infected? What use was faith when the world had already ended?

He looked at the sky. An immense shadow loomed in the dark clouds. A fleeting glimpse of something colossal and mind-breaking. And he had to avert his eyes because he was small and insignificant, unworthy to gaze upon such terrible, wondrous things.

*

Shadows encroached on the roads until there was nothing else left. Hills and fields succumbing to the dark. The sun was hidden by the tumultuous sky, and when it fell the fading of its light was barely noticed.

The coaches stopped at a rest-stop for the night. Food and drink were rationed. Prayers were said before their sparse meals. Hushed words and tones of reverence. Royce stayed silent. When he looked at their faces he saw cleft palates and hair lips, scars and disfigurements. Before the coming of the plague, most of these people would have been social outcasts. Outsiders. The Family had taken them in, welcomed and accepted them; gave their lives meaning, no matter how debatable the meaning.

George mumbled something under his breath before he started on his serving of cold spaghetti hoops and tinned pork sausages. Royce ate his food slowly, wondering how safe they were in the coaches. The windows were high above the ground, but the infected were tenacious when in pursuit of prey. He felt exposed and vulnerable.

He stared at the same moon he had watched during his boyhood. But there would be no more exploration of the solar system and beyond. He thought of the probes sent into space years ago, now drifting though the cosmos, a roaming vestige of the human race. The last memory of a dead species.

But the moon would abide, no matter what the plague did to the planet, and that made Royce feel a little better.

Later, he was drifting in and out of sleep, slipping from dreams and nightmares, groaning at his stiff legs. George was snoring. Behind him a murmured voice prayed to an obsolete god, begging for salvation.

Royce doubted reality; this world that should not be.

In his mind, a vision appeared of his wife resplendent in her wedding dress, the veil obscuring her face like a funeral shroud. He remembered a baby's cot stained with blood, toys smashed around it on the floor, and he sobbed into his hands so not to wake the dreamers around him.

CHAPTER THIRTY

A member of the Family died in the night, and was found the next morning slumped in his seat. The old man had been very ill. A few men took the body from the coach and laid it on the melting layer of snow in an empty field. The ground was too hard for them to dig a grave, and the Family didn't believe in burying the dead, so they closed his arms over his chest, raised his face to the sky and covered him in a blanket. Marek gave a short eulogy as they stood in a circle around the body and said prayers for the departed. The man's name was repeated by the mourners until Marek stopped them with a raised hand.

The infected screamed from somewhere in the distance, answering their grieving.

The body was left behind, an offering to the earth.

*

The coaches stopped periodically so that people could stretch their legs, breathe some fresh air, and relieve bladders and bowels under armed guard. The children were told to pray for guidance on the journey ahead. There were no snowball fights.

They had to bypass Salisbury because it had been bombed to shattered ruins and there was no way of going through it. It was a while before they were clear of the devastated city, crawling along bad roads through dismal villages.

Mist and drizzle, low clouds. Bouts of heavy rain that felt like punishment, lowering the visibility to about twenty yards all around. The coaches stayed together, creeping over fraying tarmac, grinding through gears.

Royce had been drifting in and out of sleep, and woke to a burst of laughter from the back of the coach. He rubbed his eyes and yawned, noticing that George was gone from his seat. Royce looked around and saw many of the Family had turned back to the rear of the bus.

George appeared in the aisle, his cheeks flushed and his mouth shaped in a hesitant smile.

"It's Amy," George said. "She says the baby's kicking."

Royce followed George to the back of the bus, where Sister Fiona had placed her hands to Amy's exposed belly. Two other women, scrawny and smirking, loitered behind her, waiting their turn. When Royce and George arrived, Amy smiled at them, tears in her eyes.

"Are you okay?" Royce asked as he crouched next to her with George. The coach's suspension rattled from potholes in the road.

"I'm fine," she said. "The baby's fine. I can't believe it, I can't believe it." Her voice was low and came out quickly. One hand hovered tentatively by her face. Her eyes were wide and near-hysterical. Muscles twitched in under her eyes and around her mouth.

"Praise God," said Sister Fiona.

Royce frowned at the old woman, but she ignored him and stared at her hands moving over Amy's stomach. "God gave the little one the strength to survive. He gave you all the strength to survive. He has a plan and you're all part of that plan. *We're* all part of the plan. He will take care of us now. Praise God."

Royce was about to reply when a booming cry from above silenced every mouth on the coach; an ear-shattering wail from gargantuan lungs and flesh caverns. Mournful. The sound of a sickly god crying into the void.

They looked to the ceiling; others peered out of the windows. The sound of the rain was like little stones falling. Royce went to a window, nudged a short man out of his way, and looked to the underside of the low cloud, as something huge within it pulsed darkly. The clouds broiled, rippling from within. Part of him thought it was beautiful. He felt a little sick.

"Is it one of those things?" George asked. No one answered him. Royce heard several people mumble frantic prayers. Shocked pale faces blurred past him as Royce went to the front of the coach. Marek's son Justin, a tall, hook-nosed man with curly hair and a slack mouth, was muttering into his walkie-talkie. His face was pale and loose-fitting.

THE LAST OUTPOST

The two coaches halted on the road. Royce held onto a handrail to avoid being pitched forward. Justin was nodding, his eyes watery, as the walkie-talkie spat Marek's voice.

"What's going on?" Royce said. "Why have we stopped?"

The driver, a sullen and wiry man, looked at the sky, and his hands tightened upon the steering wheel. Justin ignored Royce, frowning as he concentrated on the walkie-talkie. Marek's voice was jumbled by static, punctuated by strange clicks.

"Say again, Father," said Justin. He wiped sweat from his brow, staring at the front coach. "I didn't catch you. Say again, please."

Another prehistoric, reverberating cry split the sky and caused everyone on the coach to press their hands to their ears. The inside of the vehicle trembled. Someone cried out, and when Royce took his hands from his head there was the sound of something like a low pulsing in the sky. The walkie-talkie offered the sounds of children's screams, half-drowned by static. Seconds of dead silence.

The clouds were full of shadow and they were moving. Royce's heart palpitated.

"Justin…" Marek's voice on the walkie-talkie. *"Justin, we can see it above us…"* More static, like gravel falling upon metal. *"Sky…shape…immense…god…"*

Several huge black tentacles, as thick as anchor chains on cruise ships, descended from the clouds and seized the first coach, wrapping themselves around it, shattering windows and crunching sheet metal. Justin almost dropped the walkie-talkie when screams burst from its speaker. The black tentacles gripped and shook the coach, lifting it off the road. Gunshots boomed from inside the vehicle. Blurred shapes behind the rain-streaked windows. Other, thinner, tentacles dropped from the sky and coiled around the coach, puncturing metal with the pulsing spikes that burst from their skin.

"Holy fuck," said Royce. He put one hand to his mouth.

"We have to do something," Justin said, his eyes beseeching Royce. "We have to help them." He went to open the coach doors but Royce held him back.

Justin stared at Royce, his mouth quivering.

"It's too late," Royce said.

Justin pushed him away.

They turned to look out the windscreen.

The tentacles lifted Marek's coach into the air, fifty feet from the ground. The groan of metal with the snapping of rivets and bolts. A muffled bang as a tyre burst.

"You can't help them," Royce said.

Justin stared out the windscreen, his face crumpling.

The tentacles fastened and began crushing the coach. And it was taken into the sky and the clouds with its passengers. The serpentine shadows of the tentacles remained for a moment, and then they were gone. The walkie-talkie was all screams, babbling and desperate pleas from high above. A child's voice praying to God was the last thing to be heard before it went silent.

Justin stared at the walkie-talkie until Royce took it from his hands and switched it off. The rain fell against the windows, pattering softly like searching hands.

"Father," Justin said into the walkie-talkie. "Father, can you hear me?"

Royce stared at the spot where Marek's coach had been before it was snatched away. People began screaming behind him, mixing with panicked voices tight and high-pitched with fear. Some of them wailed for Marek and the children.

Justin looked at Royce, face ashen, his lips damp. His mouth moved, twitching at the corners. He slumped upon an empty seat, awestruck and trembling, and turned his face to the rain.

"They were taken," Justin said. "All those children, taken into the sky."

CHAPTER THIRTY-ONE

The coach swerved along wild country roads, the windscreen wipers struggling to keep pace with the torrential rain. People were crying, wailing and praying in despondent voices.

Royce pitied them.

The flock was lost, rudderless, unravelling. Their prayers were not answered. Some of the Family looked to him, as if for guidance, and the pain in their eyes shrivelled something inside him. Justin was staring at his hands on his lap, his head nodding faintly.

The rain didn't falter. The sound of its roaring. Staring into the rain, the driver's hands were white on the steering wheel. Royce watched above, waiting for the coach to be grabbed and plucked from the road. He thought of Marek and the others taken into the sky, and what they must have seen beyond the clouds: what those tentacles were attached to, and if there was a terrible mouth waiting for them.

The coach halted as the driver hit the brakes and the tyres screamed. Bodies fell forwards, unprepared. Royce clung to a handrail and shifted his feet so that he didn't slip on the floor. Justin hit his head on the back of the driver's seat and slumped to the floor, moaning softly with one hand to his forehead.

The driver stared through the windscreen and put his hands to his mouth. "Oh dear God. Dear God."

Royce followed his gaze and had to stifle a cry when he saw the swarm of infected ahead of the coach, lurking in the rain like an army of mourners. Hundreds – maybe thousands – of them filled the road and the fields either side for over two hundred yards in both directions. The swarm stretched away into the rain. The nearest of the infected was about twenty yards away. Most of them were facing away from the coach or staring at the ground or the sky. Drenched, ragged, emaciated. Mutated into awful things. They appeared dormant.

"What do we do now?" the driver said.

One of the infected, a woman shivering in the remains of a stained quilted housecoat, raised her face towards the coach and looked directly at Royce. She opened her mouth and her black tongue emerged and tasted the air. Then she screamed, and it pierced the falling rain and awoke those around her. The other infected turned towards the coach, their shoulders hunched, limbs twisted, spines arched or crooked, faces contorting into folds of rippling skin and flesh. Phallic growths and fleshy pincers emerged sloppily from torsos and damp clefts. Hands that grasped and flexed.

The infected shrieked, bolting towards the coach, arms flailing. Justin stood open-mouthed at the approaching swarm.

Royce looked at the driver. "Go through them."

The driver's face loosened on his skull. The first dozen infected were barely ten yards away when the driver put his foot down on the accelerator and the coach lurched forward. Royce sat down and held onto his seat.

The coach had barely hit twenty miles an hour when it collided with the swarm and was engulfed by thrashing bodies. They threw themselves at the coach, leapt at the windows, scraping and clawing at the sides until the sound of fingernails and claws upon metal was all Royce could hear above the growl of the engine and the falling rain. The coach juddered and shook as its wheels swatted and crushed bodies. The shattering of bones. Internal organs reduced to pulp. And there was no end in sight to the swarm, the bodies coming from all directions as the wheels struggled through their ranks, crunching through pulped remains. The driver twisted the steering wheel to stop the coach from crashing into a ditch.

The suspension was rattling. Some of the windows cracked, cleaved in fractures, covered in blood and gore. Infected were clinging to the coach, trying to tear at its sides. There was no way to fight them off.

The doors burst open under the pressure of the thrashing bodies. The driver lost control of the coach; it veered from the road and skidded onto wet grassland, lost to its own inertia as blood-streaked figures with gasping mouths spilled on board. They pushed the stench of gangrene and slaughter before them. Justin fired his pistol at the invaders, but the shots went wild. The infected pulled the driver from his seat and opened him on the floor. He screamed once before his voice was lost to wet splutters and his throat was torn out. Justin fired again and one of the infected fell back with a hole in its chest and bits of the driver in its mouth.

With no one to guide it, the steering wheel twisted as the coach crested the top of a slope and began to descend. The infected finished with the driver as Justin's pistol clicked empty. Two of them, naked and covered in lesions, pulsing cysts and wet wounds, jerked their horrid faces towards Royce and came at him with reaching hands.

The coach seemed to groan as it swerved with no one to control it. Metal and people screamed. Something gave way beneath the floor and the coach began leaning to one side with a terrible grinding. The snapping of pipes, precious tubes and wires. As the infected reached for Royce, the coach tipped over and the windows blew inwards and sent shards of glass through the air, piercing skin and soft faces. The blinded threw their hands to their eyes and screamed.

The last thing Royce saw was an infected man's face close to his own and blackened mouth yawning open to meet him.

CHAPTER THIRTY-TWO

Royce awoke and found himself lying amongst long yellowing grass in the pouring rain, twenty yards from where the coach had ended its journey. He had been thrown clear during the descent.

I should be dead. Why am I not dead?

He spat mud from his mouth. Moved his limbs to check they were still attached and undamaged, wincing at the grinding pain in his legs. Arms shaking, he slowly ran his fingers over his face and they came away with blood from a shallow gash under his left eye. Small cuts in his skin, under the clothes torn during his passage to the long grass. When he took a breath there was a needling pain in his torso, but he would worry later about broken ribs and internal bleeding, if he survived the next few minutes. He kept low and looked around, flinching at nearby shrieks, his vision swaying and capering, then rose to an awkward crouch and saw hundreds of infected swarming down the slope towards the crippled coach, which was a shape of torn and crumpled metal. Screams and cries came from beyond the shattered windows. Glass, metal and scraps of plastic on the ground around its stricken corpse. And there were bodies too. Some looked dead. Some of them hung limply from the windows. An injured man was trying to crawl away from the wreck, but his left leg was bent the wrong way at the knee, and his strength was fading, judging by his pathetic pawing at the muddy ground.

Royce looked for George and Amy, but from his position and distance he couldn't see them, and he couldn't tell if they were among the bodies. Maybe they had escaped and were hiding out in the fields or the nearby woods.

The infected engulfed the wrecked coach and there was no hope for those trapped inside. Survivors were pulled out and set upon, torn apart and eaten alive.

That was the last of the Family.

A sound to his left made him turn, and a bleeding face emerged from the grass. The infected man must have been thrown from the coach along with Royce. The man skittered towards him like a crab, his body broken and mutilated but still obscenely driven by the base urges to feed and infect in his diseased brain. His jaw was broken, and the lower mandibles hung loose around the tongue uncoiling from the stinking hole of his mouth, and its tip was glistening, weeping fluid, dancing slowly as if trying to mesmerise him. Royce fell onto his back and kicked out, and his foot connected with the man's face, snapping the cartilage in his nose. Gristle popped. The man fell away, hands scraping at the ground as he squealed in pain. Royce retreated on his back, slowly and painfully. His legs screamed, tender flesh and bruised skin being dragged over the earth. The grass smelled of ammonia.

The infected man came back at Royce, nose bleeding, eyes rolling into the back of his head and his breathing excited and coarse. A low whine in his throat. The muscles in his face swelled and pulsed.

The man was almost upon Royce, when his hand found a large stone and closed upon it. He thanked the rain for softening the ground so that he could prise it free. He took the stone and swung it against the side of the man's head. The man made a low grunt as the jagged face of the stone sheared the skin from his forehead, and he slumped onto one side, his writhing tongue darting at Royce's legs and narrowly missing.

Royce scrambled away, dropped the stone and rose to his feet, staggering and swaying, wiping at his face to clear blood and sweat from his eyes. A pack of infected detached from the horde and screamed on his heels. There were sounds in the sky, but he kept his eyes on the ground.

He fled into the woods, hoping to lose them among the trees, gritting his teeth and holding his left leg, hobbling on feet that felt like bleeding stumps. The pain in his ribs was immense, mind-consuming, and white-hot behind his eyes. He was close to passing out and part of him welcomed the chance to fall and let the infected take him, finally. But his legs wouldn't fail him. Through undergrowth and dense foliage, the stink of rotting wood and mammalian scents in the dirt, snagging his clothes on briar patches and thorns. Wire-thin branches scratched at his exposed face, cutting his lips and around his eyes. By the time he slumped against a lichen-blotched oak and heard the infected crashing through the trees behind him, his face was covered in fresh shallow scratches and his chest shuddered with each breath.

The infected screamed. Glimpses of movement.

Royce took hold of the low branches above his head and pulled himself up. Agony shot through his arms. His feet gained purchase on the trunk, scraping away bark and slimy moss. Then he began to climb, his weak muscles straining and hurting, and all he could think of was where to place his hands and feet to escape the infected. When he could climb no further, his arms were numb and useless and his hands were raw, he stopped and slumped upon a thick branch and wrapped his limbs around the trunk, crowded by branches jabbing and raking at him. Through the skeletal canopy he could see parts of the sky.

He pressed his face to the tree and closed his eyes.

*

Birds returned to roost in the surrounding trees as the light began fading into dusk. Royce drifted in and out of the world, finding sanctuary in exhaustion-dreams and snatches of oblivion. He was sheltered by the canopy; the threat of dying from exposure was only a peripheral blunt-toothed worry at the back of his mind.

Darkness fell.

*

During the night he woke from a nightmare he couldn't quite remember. Dream-memories of stinking maws and teeth, frenzied faces and glistening stingers. He was shivering all over and growing numb, his teeth chattering as the wind pulled at the trees. The thought of a slow death with the constellations above him. The sky was clear and full of stars, and he felt that he could touch them if he raised his arms and stretched, and then he could speak to the moon about the things it had seen. Occasionally he watched the starlit sky for the writhing of black tentacles. He didn't think about his precarious position, but he often snapped awake, terrified he was already falling. He looked beneath him, to where the ground was hidden in darkness, and he heard woodland animals upon the dead leaves and bracken. Predators and prey. The bark of a fox far away. Sounds of wild seas in the treetops. The infected were gone.

Later, in the dark hours, he thought he heard his name being called out in the woods, and he bit down on hysterical laughter. He had no time for ghosts.

CHAPTER THIRTY-THREE

At first light he climbed down the tree and rested against the base of the trunk. The descent had exhausted him as much as the climb. He clasped his empty stomach and moaned. The woods were quiet around him and the low sun hurt his eyes as he peered through the trees. The sun set fire to the horizon.

Footsteps slow and muddled, he returned to what remained of the coach and stood staring at the bodies scattered and displaced in bits and pieces around the wreck. Partially eaten corpses exposed to the dawn. Severed limbs, coils of intestine and viscera strewn about the mud. Many of the bodies were unrecognisable due to the violence of their deaths. Torn asunder and flayed. White bone sucked clean. Gnawed scraps of skin and perforated hides. The infected had fed well.

Royce looked inside the wreck and found more remains. He put his hand to his mouth when the stench hit him, and closed his eyes to the onslaught of torn, matted hair, flesh and bone. The coach was gutted, and most of the supplies were trashed but he managed to scavenge some tins of soup, baked beans, and two energy bars, one of which he ate while shivering next to a headless corpse. He put his findings in a plastic bag he found in the pocket of a dead woman's jacket.

He was searching an opened corpse when a figure appeared from behind the coach, facing away from him. Someone whom Royce recognised from the sloping of the shoulders and the tennis shoes on the small feet.

Royce didn't move.

George turned around, hunched over; his eyes were gone. The wounds on his face and neck glistened. His flayed hands made red fists. The skin visible through torn holes in his clothes was mottled with something like black rot. Royce wanted to call to him, to let him know he wasn't alone. His heart winced as he remained crouched over the corpse, hoping the smell of ripening meat would mask his own scent.

George sniffed at the air and his mouth opened to show broken teeth. He made a low sound, like an animal in distress, and turned in Royce's direction, raising his hands and forming them into claws towards his chest. The joints of his limbs twitched.

Birds lifted from nearby trees, black specks into the sky, and the sound of their wings caught the attention of the thing that used to be George. He stumbled away, palsied and famished, a vagrant monster off to roam the wasteland.

Royce watched him leave and whispered goodbye.

*

THE LAST OUTPOST

Had he believed in the Devil, he would have imagined him on those back roads, tittering at his heels and whispering over his shoulder. Royce walked without knowing where to go, taking the roads that appeared before him in the dull haze of the weak winter sun. Guilt gnawed at his stomach. He was somewhere near the town of Andover, but thoughts of his location were lost in the fog of regret and loss. He didn't care for the names of nearby towns and villages; better just to forget their names and consign them to the old world.

His head hurt and his legs only worked in small shuffling steps. He wiped at his face with hands that didn't feel like his own. As he passed a rundown chapel with a small graveyard, he turned towards the open mouth of its entrance, and the dark beyond it was filled with the sound of wet cracking and dismantling. He stood and watched the entrance for a while, hoping for something terrible to emerge from that darkness.

The coast was far away, too distant to imagine, but he had decided to keep moving east. He had no disillusions about making it and he would probably die on the way there.

Most of the day was spent walking, watching out for the horde. The sky remained clear and empty. The cold sun, the cruel sun.

He found an old stable in a field away from the road. It was a simple structure, barely big enough for two horses in its stalls. Now vermin were the only occupants, watching him from small alcoves and hidden holes. He chased the rats from the beds of rotting straw and troughs of stinking hay blighted with damp and fungi. Stirrups, saddles and martingales hanging from the walls. He found a flea-ridden blanket draped over a metal hook and laid it on the straw-covered floor of the stall that faced towards the fenced field and the tell-tale mounds of horse bones in the grass. The shapes of hills beyond were dark against the fading sky. Fire in the west. Silence across the fields. The structures of winter-jaded trees all black and sharp.

He sat on the blanket and noticed that the straw was lumpy underneath. A dried out smell, like old leather. He shifted and stood, removed the blanket. And when he pulled aside the straw he found the mummified remains of a man in similar clothes to his own. Skin like parchment, sucked of moisture, mouth agape. Royce searched the corpse and found a pack of cigarettes with a box of matches in a coat pocket. A wallet containing old photos and a Burger King coupon. Royce checked the driving license: *Ben Jones.* A square of patterned fabric, maybe from a woman's dress. Royce restored it all, except the cigarettes and matches, to the man's pockets then slowly replaced the straw upon him. Then Royce moved to the adjoining stall, but before he sat down he checked the straw on which he would make his bed.

THE LAST OUTPOST

*

He was still and silent, hidden by the ancient stink of the stable, and he fell into a deep sleep of exhaustion and regret as shadows grew over the fields.

The evicted rats did not return.

He dreamed that George visited him in the night, sat across from him on the old straw floor, and told him a story about the end of all life.

CHAPTER THIRTY-FOUR

In the morning the eaves were dripping with rain and banks of mist shrouded the hills beyond the fields. He ate half a tin of baked beans, scooping them into his mouth with his hands, and afterwards he stood in the rain and opened his face to the sky. When the rain fell harder, he retreated under the stable roof to smoke a cigarette and watch the fields. The nicotine salve in his soul couldn't stop the shaking of his hands and the palpitations in his chest. He felt diseased. When he was a boy, his Catholic grandmother had told him every person was born sick and needed absolution. The mad bitch would have seen the plague as a judgement upon the world. Lung cancer killed her. She'd died in agony, stinking of piss and whiskey.

He took a last hit from the cigarette before discarding it. Crushed it with one foot. Blue-grey smoke slipped between his teeth.

Royce was sitting on the straw, waiting out the rain, when a dog came skulking around the stable. A black and white Border collie. The animal was soaked, trembling and filthy, nervously sniffing the ground. It noticed Royce huddled in a corner of the stall, and stiffened and gave a low growl from its throat. Royce held out his hands and watched the dog. There was a collar with a tarnished name tag around its neck.

"It's okay," Royce whispered. "It's okay. I'm not going to hurt you, mate."

The dog's ears flattened. Royce forced himself to look away and not antagonise the dog by keeping eye contact. His eyes searched for something to use as a weapon. If the dog attacked, he'd be reduced to using his bare hands to fend it off. He slipped one hand into the plastic bag by his side and took out the unfinished tin of baked beans, then scooped some out with his fingers and offered it to the dog.

The dog sniffed at the air near his fingers. It took one step forwards, glancing at Royce then back at his hand.

"It's okay," Royce said. "You hungry? I bet you are hungry, aren't you?"

The dog raised and turned its head to one side, whimpering as it sensed something nearby. And before Royce could say anything, the dog turned and fled into the rain. Royce ate the beans from his fingers, gathered the plastic bag and went outside.

In the sky, several miles away, black tentacles moved like immense serpents in the clouds.

*

The rain lessened and Royce took to the road with the plastic bag clutched to his chest. Such a long time walking in the slow rain, a deathless death. Bruises swelling under his skin. The rain was pattering on the dirty sheet of tarpaulin draped over his head and shoulders. It sounded like the feet of panicking birds.

Eastwards, towards the effigy of the sun murky and frayed behind miserable clouds. There was trash on the road; aluminium cans all crumpled and empty, rolling and rattling in the wind. He kicked one and it landed in a ditch where something in a shroud of festering rags grimaced at him.

For a while he stood and cupped his hands to drink the dregs of rainwater, and then he licked the remaining moisture from the creases of his calloused palms.

*

Royce watched a flock of infected sweep across a distant hillside. The way the flock changed direction, like birds on the wing, was almost beautiful. Further on, he found a black limo parked in a layby. The engine was dead. The limo sagged on deflated tyres mired in mud and dead leaves, and when he opened one of the back doors a rancid stink hit him and he had to step back. The seats were occupied by bodies clad in expensive suits and dresses. The remains of cocaine, heroin and ketamine in little polythene bags. Dirty syringes and empty bottles of champagne, rum, gin, tequila and vodka.

A group suicide. Eight bodies, in all. A party to end all parties, while the country burned.

THE LAST OUTPOST

The bodies were skeletal, faces drawn tight over skulls and slouched postures. Vacant expressions below mops of feathery hair. Papery skin over entwined limbs and bony fingers. One of the bodies, a woman in a black strapless dress, had slumped face-first onto the lap of the man next to her. No dignity in death. The corpses were decorated with gold rings, silver necklaces, bracelets and earrings. He placed his hand around a woman's wrist so thin that his fingers completely encircled it. He imagined she had been beautiful, as he put her hand to his face so that her stick-like fingers brushed against his cheek. He looked into her face, and for a second, saw his wife. And it was too much to look into her face any longer, so he released her with a small sob, climbed out of the limo and closed the door.

*

Walking the thin lanes and roads, Royce thought he heard someone call his name, and he kept turning to check if he was being followed. The world was blurred at the edges, tinted in sepia and grey. He was warned away from a boarded-up cottage by a drunken man aiming a hunting rifle from an upstairs window.

The countryside was soaked in hues of faded brown and ash. Gleaming dew. Nothing of sustenance grew in the fields. When Royce passed a scarecrow in a black coat flapping upon its post, he remembered watching *Worzel Gummidge* on Sunday mornings, as a boy.

Ditches foaming with stinging nettles, weeds and wild flowers. Blackberry bushes without fruit. Public footpaths being absorbed slowly by the land. A tractor had been abandoned in the middle of a field.

Royce dug an ammonite fossil from the hardened topsoil. He blew away the loose dirt and ran one finger over the striations upon its coiled shape. In his youth he collected fossils and kept them in an old biscuit tin. He pocketed the ammonite and looked at the land ahead of him. No one travelled the roads. Winter trees wilted in the sunlight, crows' nests upon their bare branches. A fox darted into a copse of beeches. Tufts of sheep's wool and strips of cloth snagged on barbed wire.

Royce arrived at a shabby roadside restaurant. Out the front of the restaurant was a picnic area overgrown with weeds and an empty car park littered with trash.

He had heard the barking dog a hundred yards back down the road, and now he followed the sound of the dog along the wide ribbon of tarmac reaching behind the restaurant to another car park. A row of trees separated the property from scrubland and fields beyond.

Royce halted.

A man had tied the dog to some rusted railings once used to park bicycles. The dog strained and jerked at the knotted rope around its neck, growling at the scraggly man standing nearby with a butcher's knife in his hands. There was a small holdall on the ground by his feet. When Royce called to him, he turned and his face was severe with hunger, his shoulders thin and hunched, draped in a stained shawl. A glimpse of a dark tattoo on his throat.

Royce approached.

The man raised the knife and frowned. "What d'you want?" His beard was nicotine-stained and he kept blinking as though dust was in his eyes. A smudge of dried blood under one nostril. "Stay back."

Royce halted a few yards from the man. "What are you doing?"

The man spat, wiped his mouth and the matted hair of his beard around it. "I need to eat."

Royce nodded at the dog. "There's no meat on it."

"Better than nothing."

"No point killing a dog," said Royce.

"Who the fuck are you to say what I can eat?"

"I like dogs," Royce said. "Please don't kill the dog. I'll give you some of my food, if you want."

The man sniffed. "What you got?"

"Some chocolate. Baked beans."

The man snorted. "Baked beans? Nah. I need meat."

"If you kill and eat the dog, it'll only keep you going for a few more days. It's pointless."

"I'll just kill more dogs," the man said, and there was humour amid the desperation in his voice. "I'll kill whatever I need to survive."

Royce raised his hands in a supplicating gesture. "Please don't. There's no need to kill the dog."

The man shook his head and turned back to the struggling animal, whose whimpering broke Royce's heart. His eyes were hot and stinging, and his breathing quickened. He thought of all the dogs now feral and without families and homes, running wild and scavenging. He thought of his old dog ripped open on the front lawn and how he had watched from the kitchen window and been powerless to save him.

Royce stepped towards the man.

*

He sat in the restaurant with the knife on the table, his hands red and violent, and he couldn't shake the memory of the man's pale gasping face and blood-speckled mouth. The taking of the knife from the man's hands. The ease of the blade through the soft flesh of the throat and sawing into the windpipe. The man's pawing at him, terrified and without avail, because he was weaker than Royce.

Royce had been muttering something and he couldn't remember what the words had been. It felt like time had gone away and then returned. He had released the dog, and it had paused and watched him, then fled.

He smoked a cigarette in silence between sips from one of the bottles of water he'd found in the man's holdall. He would save the other for the road. His ribs ached, and breathing deeply brought a sharper pain that worried him. He used his tongue to nudge at loosened teeth.

After finishing the bottle, he searched the restaurant with the knife in his hand. A few sachets of tomato sauce in a plastic container next to the till. A small packet of stale biscuits beneath drifts of carrier bags. There was a wad of ten pound notes under the counter, smooth and pristine, and he put them in the stolen holdall for use as toilet paper.

He guzzled the contents of one of the sachets and pocketed the others, then searched the kitchens and the back rooms, but they had been emptied of anything edible. Frustrated, he returned to the front of the restaurant and rested at one of the tables, to look out at the man's body on the tarmac. The crows that, until recently had been lurking in the trees, were gathering around the body, and Royce wished them a wholesome meal.

His hands were shaking, and the rise and fall of his heart was erratic. Despite his guilt, killing the man had come easily to him. Just like killing the teenage boy had been a simple act.

When Royce put his head in his hands, the dead man's blood was smeared on his face.

CHAPTER THIRTY-FIVE

Later, he moved on and the dog followed him for two miles of painful walking before he stopped and turned back. The dog halted and watched him from a distance as he took one of the stale biscuits he'd found in the restaurant and held it in his hand. The dog sized up the treat, tilting its head to one side.

"Don't you remember me?"

The dog didn't move.

Royce split the biscuit and left one half on the road, turned around and moved on.

*

It occurred to Royce that maybe the dog was waiting for him to collapse so that it could attack and eat him. He kept the knife close, just in case.

The sky clouded over. Thunder far behind him. He glanced over his shoulder and saw the dog keeping pace with him at its usual distance. Later, Royce sat by the side of the road upon a muddy bank and ate sparingly from his provisions. The dog watched him from down the road, but didn't approach.

Royce took the other half of the biscuit and placed it on the road. The dog took a step forwards then stopped, looking at Royce then the small morsel by his feet.

"Good dog," Royce whispered.

The dog held its ground. Royce finished eating and continued down the road. Further on, when Royce looked back, the dog was eating the biscuit.

"Very good dog."

*

In the late afternoon Royce sheltered under the bough of an oak tree while the rain fell over the silent land. The light was fading and he would have to find somewhere to spend the night. The dog, soaked and bedraggled, sat in the rain and watched him. Royce tried to entice the dog with some food, but the dog just stared at him.

Royce put the food away and huddled against the tree. "Stupid dog."

*

When the rain stopped and the only sounds were from water sluicing into flooded drainage ditches and dripping from trees, Royce moved on and the dog followed him.

A village appeared in the dying light. The spire of a church as a warning or a welcome. There was only silence, but he didn't trust it. Approaching the village, he stopped and wiped months' worth of grime from the sign at the side of the road.

St. Mary Bourne. He was somewhere in Hampshire.

Below the sign was an arrangement of small bones. A cairn of remains, including a child's skull with the cranium smashed. Next to it was a glass jar full of milk teeth. What would George have said about it? What did it mean? He tried not to ponder too much as he entered the silent village and stepped among shattered glass and derelict cars. Everything dull with the coming of dusk. Pools of black forming as the light fell away. He took out the knife. There was a corpse propped upright in a bus shelter, a peeled man grinning at Royce's arrival.

He stopped in the middle of the street, his hands at his sides, breathing in the damp air. Nothing emerged from the houses, the quaint shops or the overgrown gardens. But the darkness within the open doorways and windows was thick and pulsing, and he gripped the knife a little tighter.

*

The stink of rot and decay pushed away from some houses, and he didn't want to see the corpses waiting for him inside those charnel rooms. Maybe in the morning, when his resolve was a little stronger and the dark wasn't so keen on his shoulders. He chose a house that appeared uninhabited and watched the windows as drizzle fell upon him, waiting for the twitch of a net curtain or a shadow behind the glass. The front door was ajar, showing a sliver of darkness, and he walked up the garden path past a child's tricycle fading into the high grass. The smell of mildew came to him when he pushed the door open. He hesitated on the threshold and checked the hallway walls for claw marks or blood. The carpet was waterlogged where the rain had entered through the doorway. He listened and frowned, aware of a scraping sound from the kitchen, ahead of him. Royce breathed slowly through his mouth.

The child emerged from the kitchen, infested with pus-filled tumours, and almost fell into Royce's arms. He pushed it away as he raised the knife in his other hand, and felt no horror when he looked into the thing's face. Only a deep sadness manifesting in his bones. The plague had made the child genderless and shrivelled, naked and hairless, rasping through the dripping hole of its mouth. Its eyes, glazed and sore, their sockets raw with lesions and scratches that leaked milky discharge, appraised Royce. It stank of sewage and decay.

When the child fell upon the knife it simply gasped and collapsed, palsied limbs trembling in its death throes. Royce looked at its face and was certain he saw relief.

He stayed with the child until it died.

*

On the outskirts of the village he found a house clean of infection. He checked the rooms and the hiding places, under the beds and in the airing cupboard. And when he was finished he secured the house from the inside as best he could and stood by one of the windows observing the street. There was no sign of the dog, and he hoped it had found somewhere safe for the night.

He closed the curtains, then lit a candle and acquainted himself with the silence of the house's empty rooms. A painting of a scene from Dante's *Inferno* mounted over the blackened fireplace. Stacks of old science journals in a corner. Cushions thrown around the floor. On a pinewood table, a pile of textbooks about quantum mechanics. He flicked through the pages until his eyes began to hurt, the pages beyond his comprehension. It was lost knowledge, anyway, unless there were still scientists hiding somewhere, maybe in a lab in some secret bunker.

He walked through the rooms of the house and tried not to dwell upon the photos on the walls.

*

Royce found a bottle of TCP and a batch of cotton buds in the cabinet above the bathroom sink. Sitting on the edge of the bath, he dabbed at the many cuts and scratches on his body, gritting his teeth against the pain. But the pain soon faded and when he finished he drank from the dusty bottle of red wine he'd scavenged from the back of a kitchen cupboard. Dark bruises on his skin. One of his molars dropped from his gums and he spat it into the toilet bowl, where its bloody root reddened the water.

"Falling apart," he said, and threw more wine down his neck.

His back seized up soon afterwards, and he spent the rest of the night sprawled on the sofa with the bottle to his lips.

He heard infected in the street outside and waited for them to arrive at his door.

*

His dreams were violent with reds, death-screams and spasms. The screams of everyone he'd lost. Snatches of memory from stumbling through a street with police sirens about him and people dead in the gutters. Low concussions from nearby streets. Running for his life with monsters on his heels, his cries slipping through the smoke of house-fires. A burning church from which flaming shapes emerged shrieking. A soldier in a gas mask and tactical armour gunning down fleeing civilians. The tune of his daughter's favourite toy playing over the madness of the outbreak. The memory of cowering behind a wheelie bin when a pack of infected set upon an old man. Flocks of birds reeling into the air as the infected screamed down avenues and roads, attacking the cars stuck in traffic jams, swarming those who tried to escape. Windows smashed and shattered and doors were torn away by the ravenous things. Slaughter on the roads. The chaos spreading. Blood on the streets. A man dragging a girl into an alleyway. Royce's feet treading on something soft and damp, but he didn't look down. Never look down.

He heard George's voice amidst the panic and death, calling to him, calling for help. But there was no help to be given, or to be had, and no way to change what had gone before.

The dead would remain dead.

CHAPTER THIRTY-SIX

He woke on the sofa and whispered his wife's name. What day was it? He coughed through what felt like a mouthful of ash, and his teeth tasted of blood and old wine. He groaned and rubbed his face then put one hand to his damaged ribs and dry heaved into a wicker wastepaper bin he'd grabbed from the floor. The tune from his daughter's favourite toy was stuck inside his head. He remembered he used to press the red button on the teddy bear's stomach and it would sing a nursery rhyme in a funny voice. The bear had annoyed him to the point where he'd tried to discreetly dispose of it in the bin at the end of the garden, but now he would have given his teeth, eyes and toes just to hold the bear and smell it and recognise the marvellous scent of his daughter's skin imbued within it.

*

He scavenged some items from the house, including a can of lemonade he drank in one go to dull the raging thirst in his mouth and throat. The front door was too loud as it opened. He stood with the cold air against his face as a songbird warbled in a nearby garden in the first hours of daylight.

The dog was watching him from the footpath, crouching on its back legs.

Royce paused in the doorway. "Good morning. Want some breakfast?"

That the dog didn't run was an affirmative answer, Royce reckoned. He went into the kitchen and rooted through the cupboards and drawers until he found a can of dog food he'd spotted yesterday. He emptied it into a cereal bowl then placed it just inside the front doorway.

The dog watched intently. Pricked up its ears then rose from path and stood glancing back-and-forth between Royce and the bowl. Sniffed at the air and stepped forward, ribs moving under its hide. Royce retreated from the bowl until he was in the doorway of the living room down the hallway from the front door. The dog entered the house slowly and looked around. Its long claws scratched on the carpet as it went to the bowl and sniffed at the food. A moment of hesitation, in which Royce was sure the dog would turn and flee; but then it was taking mouthfuls of the soggy mush. It was ravenous. The poor starving thing.

Royce watched the dog, arms folded, and waited until it had finished the meal before he stepped forward, but the dog turned and ran from the house. And before Royce was halfway down the garden path, the dog had disappeared into wild gardens down the street, and he would be lucky to see it again.

THE LAST OUTPOST

*

Before Royce left the village he searched the grocery shop and found a can of Happy Shopper orangeade underneath a mess of torn cardboard and plastic wrapping, dented and scuffed but airtight. He also scavenged a few tins of corned beef right on the edge of their expiry dates, and while searching a garden he picked up an axe and a folding spade from a ramshackle shed left unlocked by its last owners. He swung the axe and the weight in his hands felt proper and good.

He left the village and looked for the dog in the fields, but there was no sign of it and he accepted he was alone except for the rain and wind following him along the road.

He walked, one foot then the other, over and over.

A field of scrubland, bracken and stinking mud was a graveyard for over a dozen army tanks left abandoned during the outbreak. The ground was scarred and pitted, bullet casings gleaming in the mud. Royce walked among the tanks and counted fourteen rusting hulks in the rain. Dripping barrels and turrets. He trod over bones sinking into the mud and over patches of ground scorched bare, broken by craters and rents. On the other side of the field, something with multiple black insect legs hunched over a mound of carrion, pulsing intermittently. There were other things crawling over the ground. Things that skittered and cried and scuttled and howled. Creatures made of tendrils, with human faces screaming from amongst folds of blubbery flesh. Pale-limbed beasts thrashing in the mud. Scavengers of rot.

Royce kept low and slipped away before the monsters saw him.

*

The dual carriageway stretched away from him and found the horizon. The rain had ceased. Royce stepped between left-behind vehicles fading into the same dull shades as the road. Crows flapped around a collapsed tent on the central reservation. His boots scraped damply on the layer of leaf-mulch covering the road and he hefted the axe with both hands, glancing at the bits of rubbish accumulated beneath the vehicles. The bonnets and roofs of some cars were coated in dead leaves and muck.

He watched flocks of birds in distant skies, and was caught unaware by an infected woman in a stained and shredded tracksuit as she climbed from the front of a car and lurched towards him on bare feet all raw and flayed. Serrated teeth unsheathed from putrid gums, awash in black fluid spilling down her chin. She was all sharp edges and glistening meat, gibbering and wheezing past raw lips formed in something like a pout. Royce pushed her away with the sole of his foot and when she came back at him he swung the axe in a wide horizontal swipe and caught her in the side of her neck. Her head lolled to one side with a wet snap and something cracked underneath her skin. She made a pained gurgling as Royce hit her again and she fell against the car and cracked a window with the back of her head.

"I'm sorry," Royce said.

She was slumped on the tarmac with her arms raised to him when he stepped towards her and brought down the axe. And when he was finished with her, he searched amongst the cars while he watched for other surprises. In the back of an old Vauxhall he found – among scattered comic books, glassware and useless electronic gadgets – a plastic bag swollen with lottery scratchcards. He sat on the front seat and went through them, scraping at the cards with the nail of his index finger. He laughed when he scratched away the varnish over the numbers on the fifteenth card in his hands and realised he had won ten thousand pounds. He laughed until his throat ached and his stomach cramped. And for a while he couldn't stop laughing and he didn't care; didn't care for it any more than he cared for the insects crawling over the upholstery or the rats watching him from the roadside gutters.

He stood and threw the scratchcards onto the road and they scattered in the wind.

*

Royce kept walking with his face against the wind. He sometimes thought that George was behind him, keeping him company on the road. No movement in the fields to either side. He watched the horizon and pulled his coat tighter around his throat. He stopped when he noticed something under a slumping tree at the side of the road. A damp mound of black and white fur that fell into focus when he came nearer. Something dead.

He stood over the body of the dog and bowed his head. Closed his eyes as his heart shrivelled. The pain of his empty stomach; a tremendous sadness inside him that rose into his chest and took the breath from his lungs.

The dog was curled up as if sleeping, head resting on its front paws. Royce crouched and laid his hand on the dog's head and there was no warmth. He looked for a cause of death, but there was none. Dehydration or starvation, maybe. Royce checked the loose collar around its thin neck. A metal tag with a name and a telephone number.

Freddie.

Maybe Freddie had known death was coming and had come here to die. Royce stroked the dog's fur and whispered to him and hoped he had passed without pain or sadness.

He hoped Freddie hadn't felt too alone.

*

Using the spade, Royce dug a shallow grave in a field away from the road, then lowered the dog into the earth with much care and piled the excavated dirt upon the body and recited a poem about death his paternal grandfather had often quoted when drunk. The wind took the words and dried his mouth, and he stared at the damp ground with his face slack and tired.

Royce gathered stones from nearby and piled them atop the grave. He stood next to the grave and looked out across the countryside, feeling like the last warden of an old world. He was wishing he could have saved the dog, when a series of gunshots rang out far ahead, down the road.

*

He walked, watching the distance ahead and blinking rain from his eyes. A low pain settled at the top of his skull and began to work downwards. His bones were heavy and slow, a skeleton in filthy clothes shambling along a blackened road. Pain all over him like hard fingers. A ghoul haunting the highways.

There was a traffic pile-up ahead, and when he arrived there with his legs aching and his pulse pounding in his ears, he found the bodies of two infected slack and dead upon the road. A man and a woman, starvation-thin and covered in grime, their chests opened from fresh gunshot wounds. The woman's stomach was riddled with pale tendrils. The man had died with his hands grasped into claws resting upon his chest.

The sound of movement behind him, but before he could turn, something cold and hard was pressed against the back of his head. A metallic click trembled through his skull. A gun, he thought absently, relieved that his end would be quick. But he recognised the voice that ordered him to raise his hands and turn around.

He pivoted with his hands in the air. The tip of the pistol barrel inches from his head.

Sister Fiona's face was gaunt and sickly, her hair matted with dried filth. Her pistol hand was shaking and her finger quivered upon the trigger. She frowned, uncertainty in her eyes, her mouth closed and bloodless and mean.

"Royce?" Her voice wavered.

He nodded, remained still, and he didn't lower his hands until she lowered the gun.

Sister Fiona called over her shoulder: "You can come out. It's safe."

A small face rose from behind a dead car beyond the old woman. Nervous eyes. Then the face broke into a sad, strained smile. Amy emerged from her hiding place, cradling her stomach in her hands. She went to Royce and hugged him, and he could do nothing but stand there and feel her face buried against his chest.

CHAPTER THIRTY-SEVEN

The housing estate had been built less than a year before the world ended. Red brick modern houses arranged in small cul-de-sacs where the new roads and pavements terminated. Houses in straight rows along empty streets. Now the gardens were dense and flourishing with weeds, but the roads were remarkably clean, as if the apocalypse hadn't touched the estate. No cars on the roads or the driveways. Some of the FOR SALE signs had collapsed. The windows of the houses were bare, and it occurred to Royce that the estate wasn't inhabited when the outbreak hit. He looked through double-glazed windows into unfurnished rooms with bare walls.

Amy and Sister Fiona stood in the street, huddled together in the vanishing light.

*

Royce chose a house at one end of a cul-de-sac and gained entry through a side door. They searched the house and then settled in the living room, whose window looked out onto a walled-in garden. The wall was high enough to hide any light in the window from anyone outside the property. Royce went out into the back garden and tested the wooden gate, which held and was almost as tall as the wall.

Candles were lit and blankets were laid out next to tins of food. The sagging and slumping of limbs. Tired breaths. Exhaustion in the words taken from their mouths.

They shut themselves away from the world, sat with the candle between them, and the light painted their shadows upon the walls. The room still retained the smell of plaster. They were shivering in their blankets, solemn faces in the candlelight. Pitch black past the window, night without starlight, absent moon. Absolute darkness. They ate the food they could spare for that night, all of it taken in small mouthfuls in the silence of the room. Royce swigged from the can of orangeade and wiped the back of his sleeve over his mouth. His beard itched.

"How did you survive?" Royce asked the women. "Did anyone else make it?"

Sister Fiona looked at him then looked away quickly and folded her arms over her chest. Amy raised her face from the candle flame; her eyes could have been oil. "We were still inside the coach when the infected swarmed us. Everything seemed at weird angles; it was unreal and dream-like. There was blood and broken glass. It felt like someone had been kicking me. Some people were already dead, but most were injured. The infected dragged people through the shattered windows, and some infected were clawing to get inside. I remember their faces, and I remember the faces of the people around us. Some of them prayed, but it didn't do them any good." Amy gently rubbed her belly, her eyes distant. "Fiona grabbed my hand and took care of me. We managed to get out by crawling through the busted fire escape at the back of the coach. Fiona shot some infected that came at us and she dragged me with her until we were clear of the crash site. We hid amongst the trees, and when I looked back towards the coach, I didn't see anyone else escape. Fiona saved my life and my baby's life."

Royce looked at her and imagined those terrible minutes inside the wrecked coach.

Amy wiped her eyes. "How did you escape, Royce?"

He told them about how he had been thrown clear and spent the following hours hiding up a tree.

"What happened to George?" Amy said. "I didn't see him."

Royce swallowed. "He's dead." A lie was a kinder gift than the truth.

"You saw him?"

"Yes. He died quickly, if that helps. He didn't suffer."

Amy nodded, then winced and held her stomach.

"The baby?" Sister Fiona asked her.

"She's just kicking." Amy tried to smile, but it was very thin. She squeezed her eyes shut, and when she opened them again she exhaled through gritted teeth and touched the small of her back. "The little monkey is playing football, I think. Maybe she'll play for England Ladies one day. She's a tough one, I can tell."

"Just like her mother."

"I keep worrying she'll be born prematurely," Amy said. "All this stress, fear and exhaustion."

Sister Fiona placed one wrinkled hand on Amy's shoulder. "She'll arrive when she's ready."

Amy looked at the candle flame. Her eyes were large and glassy. "I wonder how long until she's ready."

"Are *you* ready?" said Royce.

She raised her face to him. "Yes. She's the reason I've come this far. She's the only reason I'm alive – to bring her into the world."

"You'll be a fine mother, Amy," said Sister Fiona. "You'll keep her safe."

"Do you think we'll reach the coast?" Amy said.

Sister Fiona sipped her water. "Have faith, Amy."

Amy nodded, blinking her moist eyes.

Royce looked at the women's shadows on the wall. "We should get some sleep. We all need some rest. Tomorrow will be a long day."

*

Amy was asleep, wrapped in her blankets so only her face was exposed. Royce watched her during the night, when he couldn't sleep because of the images that visited him whenever his closed his eyes. Horrid faces and awful mouths. Sister Fiona had left the room to walk around the house. Royce went to find her.

She was standing at an upstairs window looking out at the deserted street. The clouds had parted and the moon was out. The pale light made her a ghost. She glanced at Royce when he stood next to her, but said nothing.

They stared out at the night.

"I'm sorry about your group," said Royce.

She looked at the moon. "Thanks. That's very kind of you to say."

"You should get some sleep."

"They're all gone," she said. "Taken up. I've lost them all. I don't know why God would let that happen. Did He do it to save them from suffering? But if that's true then why did He leave me here? Did I commit a sin, or offend God? What did I do? Am I forsaken, Royce?"

He wanted to tell her that he thought it was all nonsense, but he didn't have the heart. "Things just happen. We can't stop that."

"Everything happens for a reason."

"I don't believe that."

"You don't believe in anything, Royce. I knew that when you travelled with us."

"So, if everything happens for a reason, why did your god let the plague decimate the planet?"

"Punishment, I think."

"And I'm guessing that you and your group thought you were spared God's wrath because of what you believed? Is that what you told all the children?"

"Yes. Because it was true. We were His chosen people."

"So why are the rest of them dead?"

Fiona's breath was mist on the window. "I don't know. It's not for me to understand God's work. Maybe He has left me in this world as a lesson…because I was too pious, too sure of myself. I don't know. I prayed for a sign, for an answer, but there's nothing."

Royce folded his arms, watched the stars pulsate and shimmer. He didn't know what to say.

"I don't want to stay here any longer," she said. "I want to leave."

"We'll leave in the morning," Royce said.

"No, you misunderstand. I want to leave this world, this life."

"You want to die?"

"I want to die."

"Don't say that. You can't leave Amy and the baby."

"That's why I'm glad we found you again," she said. "Because now I can leave and be sure you'll take care of them. I couldn't have left them alone in this terrible world. But now you're here, Royce, and you can be their guardian."

"No, wait…"

THE LAST OUTPOST

She offered him the pistol. Her face was serene. "I want you to shoot me, Royce."

"I can't do that." He stepped back and held his hands in front of him. "I won't."

"Please," she said. "It would be a kindness. I want to join my people – my brothers and sisters – in the next world. Don't make me stay here alone."

"You're not alone," Royce said. "You've got me and Amy."

"Yes, and I'm thankful to both of you. But you're not my family. You're not my people. I have to be with my people. Don't you understand?"

"I'm sorry, but I can't," Royce said. "There's enough death around here."

Sister Fiona turned away and looked out at the darkness. The pistol remained in her hand.

"A little more death won't make any difference."

*

Royce woke on the floor with the echoes of bad dreams crying in his head. There had been a nightmare about Amy giving birth to a squealing thing with claws and hooves.

A noise had woken him. He lay still. It had been the sound of a door closing. Amy was still asleep. Sister Fiona's heavy coat was bundled on the floor, next to her pistol. Royce listened for the sound of movement in the house, but he could only hear Amy's gentle breathing across from him.

He rose and stumbled into the hallway. The front door was shut. He went into the kitchen and stood among the bare worktops and empty cupboard units, his heart loud and stuttering. Looking out the window he saw Sister Fiona walking up the road away from the house, towards the other end of the cul-de-sac.

He checked on Amy to make sure she was still asleep, then grabbed the pistol and went outside, where he glimpsed the old woman disappearing around the side of the last house at the far end. He staggered after her, breathing hard and wincing at the stiff joints in his legs, boots scuffing on the unbroken tarmac. From a garden, birds took flight into a reddening sky. Royce rounded the corner of the last house and halted.

The estate ended, and beyond the last house Sister Fiona was walking away across a field, approaching a long ridge of tall trees. Royce broke into a pained jog, gaining upon her, but when he was within fifty yards of her and she was on the edge of the treeline, she halted and turned to face him.

Royce stopped.

Sister Fiona was shaking her head.

"Come back," Royce said.

No, she mouthed, and her face was serene.

The infected flooded from the trees behind her, festering, crooked and frenzied. Swiping claws and jabbering mouths. She turned to accept them with her arms held wide.

CHAPTER THIRTY-EIGHT

Royce staggered back to the estate. He reached the house and his legs gave out and he slumped in the garden, his breath spilling out of him. The front door was open, but he was sure he'd closed it before going after Sister Fiona. He went into the house and called to Amy, but there was no response and he hurried into the living room and her bag was still on the floor along with her discarded blankets. He called her name again, searched the house then outside.

She was gone.

He searched deeper into the estate, wandering into a stretch of woodland that bordered the road to the east. Infected people milled about between the trees, wheezing and growling, slouching in the dead leaves, bracken and muck. He retreated back the way he'd come when something made of sharp limbs and tendrils thrashed through the foliage near to where he'd been hiding.

He circumnavigated the estate, but found no sign of Amy, and he stood in the middle of the street with his hands on the top of his head. Turned to look at the houses around him as tears welled in his eyes. Saliva on his lips. Chest shivering with his ragged breathing.

From the field where Sister Fiona had been slaughtered, the infected screamed.

*

Royce sat on the floor of the living room with his back to the wall, facing the window with the pistol in both hands. There were four bullets left. He stared past the window at the patch of sky and watched it dim as hours passed in the waning day. He did not eat or drink and he closed his eyes for minutes at a time when he tried to remember the faces of his family and all the friends he had lost. He remembered George, and cried for the old man and his cruel fate.

Time passed. Thunder in distant skies. The walls were flawless and cold around him and he was alone again. Always alone to face the dark.

Time passed.

Three knocks at the front door woke him from his stupor. His heart lurched as he listened. Another three knocks, slow and deliberate, like knuckles rapping on his coffin lid.

He got to his feet, checked the rounds in the pistol, and went to answer the door.

*

He stepped outside and raised the pistol, but there was no one waiting for him, so he walked into the road and looked both ways along the empty street.

THE LAST OUTPOST

The breeze muttered and the hairs rose on the back of his hands. He swallowed, shifting his feet as he looked around, and he thought he saw movement down one end of the close, but it'd only been a piece of paper flapping across the road in the wind.

Thunder echoed from far away.

He knew he wasn't alone even before he turned around. He pivoted, kept the pistol raised, and his finger trembled on the trigger.

Twenty yards away, in the middle of the road, a man held Amy at gunpoint, standing behind her with his arm hooked around her neck and her pistol to the side of her head. Her wrists were bound with rope and she was weeping, her eyes puffy and reddened. Her mouth quivered when she looked at Royce.

The man was clad in a dirty trench coat and torn jeans. Greasy hair scraped back from his brow. His face was scratched and raw amidst the patchy beard. He was biting his lip, staring at Royce with such unbridled hate that he felt his insides shrivel and wane.

"Put down your gun," the man said to Royce, his voice matter-of-fact and emotionless.

Royce didn't move. He looked at Amy. Her downcast eyes, exhausted and terrified, and the pleading shape of her mouth.

"Put down your gun," the man repeated. "Or she dies. It's your choice."

"Who are you?" Royce said. "What do you want?"

"Do what I say. Put down the gun."

"Has he hurt you, Amy?" Royce kept his eyes on the man's face.

Amy shook her head.

"What do you want?" Royce asked the man.

"I want you," the man said.

"What?"

"You heard me. Put down the fucking gun. If you don't, she'll die and it'll be your fault. More blood on your hands."

"Don't hurt her," Royce said. "Don't do anything stupid. Just tell me why you're doing this."

The man's grin was severe, bitter and wolfish. "You don't remember?"

"Remember what…?"

"The teenage boy you shot. You were hiding in a ditch when he found you and you shot him. You killed him."

Royce remembered. A sharp memory of the lad's shocked face as the buckshot tore into him. The blood on the ground.

"He was my younger brother," the man said.

Royce tried to speak, but the muscles in his mouth were slack, and the sky suddenly felt very low. The world closing in.

"I remember," said Royce. Words formed slowly from his dry mouth. "I'm sorry, but I didn't have a choice. I thought he was going to kill me. I thought you were hunting us."

The man shook his head. "We were heading for the east coast. We'd heard packs of infected in the local area, so we were in formation in case they attacked. I'd already lost two men the day before."

"Your men?"

"I was their leader. But now they're all gone. Most of them are dead, killed by the infected. The others abandoned me to make their own way across the country when I told them I was going to track you down."

"You've been tracking us, all this time?"

"My brother was only seventeen."

"I didn't want to kill him. If I could live that moment again, I'd change what I did. I'm sorry."

"I have no intention of hurting the lady or her unborn child, as long as you comply. I'm not a monster and I have no quarrel with them. All you have to do is put down your gun and I'll let them go."

"How do I know you'll keep your promise?"

"If I'd wanted to hurt her, I'd have already done it. This isn't about her; it's you I want. Now do as I say. This doesn't have to get ugly."

Royce felt his heart sag like old cloth. His arms could scarcely hold the weight of the pistol. He blinked at the heat in his eyes. The regret and melancholy that would never leave him. His head hurt, and such a feeling of exhaustion fell over him that it was all he could do to stay on his feet.

He looked at the pistol in his hands, then at Amy. Finally, at the man. "Okay."

"No, Royce, don't…" Amy's voice was small and frightened.

"Shut up," the man told her, and he tightened his grip around her neck.

Slowly, Royce raised his hands and threw the pistol into a garden, so it was lost among the long grass. He put his hands at the back of his head.

The man let go of Amy and pushed her away, then he was upon Royce in several quick steps, and Royce held up his hands but it did no good. The man batted away Royce's frail defensive gesture and fell upon him with his fists until he was curled up on the ground. And then the man began with his feet, kicking Royce's stomach, groin and legs, and he never said a word. Agony exploded over Royce's body as he tried to fold himself small to deflect the man's attack, but those hard fists and feet found his soft parts and bones and ripped the breath from his lungs. He felt bones crack and skin tear, and the world became blinding, white-hot pain when a boot caught him in the back of the head.

Amy screamed and tried to pull the man away from Royce's cowering form, but the he pushed her to the side of the road and when she tried again, the raising of the pistol discouraged her and she kept her distance.

The man halted and looked down at Royce. He stepped away, wiping his mouth. Sweat glistened on his forehead.

"Get up," the man said.

Gradually, Royce unfurled himself, still shielding his torso with his elbows as he coughed into his bruised hands. Crumpled upon the road, his body sore and raw, and his insides felt fractured, loosened into broken bits. His ears rang. Fresh bruises rising on his skin. The healing cuts and wounds from the coach crash were reopened and bleeding. He leaned to one side and vomited a pale fluid flecked with blood onto the road. One of his front teeth tumbled past his lips and fell into the vomit. He raised his head, and the sky was too bright and the ground seemed to rise and fall. After he'd wiped his wet lips and purged the last of the vomit from his mouth, he looked up at the man, cowering like a beggar, his hands near his head and shaking.

The man's face was morose, heartbroken, and the hand by his side was curled into a bloodless fist. He nodded towards Amy. "Say goodbye to her. I'll let you have that." He stepped away and let Amy go to Royce. She crouched by his side and held his shoulders as Royce sat up. He wheezed and groaned, grimacing at fresh agonies in his limbs. With one push of his tongue he found more loosened teeth.

Falling apart at the end of it all.

The man lowered his pistol and watched them.

Royce coughed when he tried to speak, and it took a while for the spasms in his chest to subside. His eyes watered and wetted the darkening bruises on his face, and he told Amy that he was sorry he couldn't stay. She was crying, and she hugged him and he savoured her warmth, the smell of her hair. Her life and the life within her.

With his free hand, Royce wiped a tear from her cheek.

"Hurry up," the man said behind them, rubbing his sore knuckles.

Royce wished Amy and the baby well and told her to keep heading for the east coast.

"Fiona's dead, isn't she?" said Amy.

"The infected. It was quick. I saw it happen."

"I thought we were going to stay together. All of us."

"Things don't always work out the way we want them to," Royce said. He doubled over into a coughing fit, clutching his ribs.

"I don't know if I can make it on my own," Amy said. Her face was very close to his. She was trembling.

Royce shook his head and tried to smile for her. "Yes, you can. You're stronger than you think you are. You're stronger than me. You don't need me, Amy. Find sanctuary, be safe and stay resolute. You'll be a wonderful mother."

She looked at him, her body terribly frail underneath her clothes, her face blotchy and wet. She said nothing, wiped under her eyes.

"Did you have any names in mind for the baby?" Royce said.

"I don't know. Why?"

He told her a name.

"I quite like it," she said. "Why that name?"

"It was my daughter's name. She should be remembered somehow."

Amy was nodding, her face creasing into a stifled sob.

"It's going to be okay," Royce said. "Look at me. You'll make it to the last outpost."

"Let's go," the man said. "Get up."

Amy helped Royce to his feet, and he groaned with each movement in his throbbing, sore joints. Her hands were a comfort upon him. When she let go of his shoulders he wavered and held his arms out to stay upright. The sky pulsed when he looked at it. He stepped away from Amy, and she made to follow him, but the man with the gun forced her back. She bristled and opened her mouth to say something, but Royce looked at her and shook his head.

"It's okay," Royce told her. "It'll be okay." His words tasted of blood.

The man jabbed the pistol towards Royce, forcing him down the road. "Maybe you'll see each other in the next world."

With the man at his back, Royce started walking down the road. One foot, then the other. Boots scraping. The man's slow breathing behind him. Crows perched in treetops, cawing at a condemned man.

Royce never looked back.

CHAPTER THIRTY-NINE

They went into the fields, the man walking three paces behind Royce, their slow footfalls on the damp earth under a sky like a sea of ash. Royce kept his hands raised and looked straight ahead, hunched over and swaying in the rain-specked wind. With each breath came a sharp pain in his chest. His ribs grinding on broken angles. One side of his face was swollen, his left eye half-closed and weeping, and the cuts and bruises on his body leeched at the last of his strength. He was ready to fall down.

"You understand why I must do this," said the man.

"I understand," Royce said.

"A life for a life, like the old ways," the man said. "I wish there was another way, but you've left me no choice."

"Please don't hurt Amy, after this, once you've finished with me."

"I have no intention of hurting her; I'll be heading up north once we're done here."

"What's up north?"

"I've always wanted to visit the Lake District. Never had the chance to go before. My wife always preferred to go abroad."

"You were married?"

"She was infected during the outbreak. I had to kill her."

"Sorry to hear that."

"There was no other choice."

"Do you remember her face?" said Royce.

"Most of the time," the man said. "It's difficult some days, like I can see her through a veil."

"You're lucky. I can't remember my wife's face, or my daughter's."

The man spat. "It's all fading into the dark."

"I hate the dark."

"It's all around us. The dark always wins, don't you think? I think we'll all be gone soon."

"Maybe," Royce said. "Depends how many of us are left." His thoughts drifted to Amy, and he tried to imagine her raising her child in a world of monsters.

"I don't see where we go from here," the man said. "The plague is everywhere. I used to think we could reach the stars, and make great discoveries. What we could have achieved. But maybe it was never to be, and the plague is just the universe's way of wiping us from existence. Maybe we've had our time in the sun. We never thought it could happen to us. Just think how many species have died out in the history of our planet. Lost to time. Millions of species. It's beyond comprehension. We're just another one to add to the list. An ape that grew too clever for its own good. But the Earth will abide."

"Do you find that comforting?" Royce asked him.

"In a way. I don't know what will happen to the infected. Maybe they'll die out, or go dormant. Maybe they'll evolve into something else."

They walked on. Meadows forming out of the wild fields. Birds in the sky, weaving flocks. The bleak call of something in the woods.

They arrived at a stretch of barren ground and the man told Royce to stop and kneel down. Royce complied, wincing at the pain in his legs, one hand over his fractured ribs. His heart was steady. There was no fear of death, not now. He was beyond that. He stared straight ahead as the man moved closer behind him. The wind slipped across the fields and the broken horizon. The dead towns and villages, and the ruined cities.

Royce looked at the wane of the light in the clearing sky; the last time he'd see the sun as it fell. Taking his last breaths with the taste of blood and dirt in his mouth.

The man put the pistol to the back of Royce's head and his breath caught in his throat. Royce looked out across the fields towards a hedgerow where the arrangement of rags and sticks could have passed for the forms of his wife and his swaddled daughter. Waiting for him to join them. Pleasing shapes to ease the last act of a life. It was easy to fool himself, especially now, even after all he'd seen.

The man let out a tired breath. "You won't hear the shot." His voice was almost kind.

THE LAST OUTPOST

Royce closed his eyes, and he smiled when he delved back into past years and finally remembered the faces of his family.

"I want to go home."

And the man was right; Royce never heard the shot.

CHAPTER FORTY

The car had broken down five miles from the coast, rattling to a stop on a wind-blown stretch of some derelict road. Now she was walking, her bag hanging from her shoulder, the pistol in her hand tucked inside one pocket. The memories of Royce, George and Sister Fiona travelled with her. She pulled her coat over her swollen belly and pushed on, breathing through a clenched jaw at the aches and pains bursting within her limbs.

Sometimes, when she concentrated, she thought she could almost smell the sea.

She had last seen an infected person two days ago. The nights were silent without their cries. She wondered if they were dying out, with nothing left to prey upon and winter in its coldest months.

Amy looked ahead to the distant horizon, where huge banks of black clouds had formed to the east, out to sea. Falling drifts of distant rain like a veil over the sky.

The road never seemed to end, and she walked on.

Her water broke as she struggled along a dirt track on the outskirts of another unnamed village. She stumbled to a barn in a nearby field and shut herself inside and slumped on a blanket she laid upon the straw pile at the back of the building. Meagre daylight slipped through the thin gaps between the wooden slats in the walls. She pulled off her boots and her jeans then placed Royce's pistol at her side.

The contractions were like knives slashing inside her. She felt like she was coming apart. The world was white-hot agony, and she screamed and cried, writhing, sweating and squirming on the blanket. The pain deepened, spread, and she cried and shut her eyes so she wouldn't have to look at the shifting walls and heaving floor.

The time shortened between the contractions until she felt the baby move and she was ready to push.

She opened her eyes. Her swollen breasts ached. Fire inside her. Immense pain beyond anything she'd ever felt before. The smell of her insides. Blood and fluids leaking onto the blanket. The urge to expel everything from her body. She snatched handfuls of straw and clenched her hands into fists.

A lone infected, drawn by her screams, was scratching at the exterior walls and the door, trying to get in. Glimpses of its awful face sniffing between the slats. It growled and shrieked, enraged in its hunger, tortured by bloodlust. Amy shouted and cursed at the creature.

"Go away! Leave me alone!"

The baby emerged after the sun had gone down, squirming and grey, bloodied and gore-streaked. A screaming girl. Amy lit a Coleman lantern from her pack and then cut the newborn's umbilical cord with a pair of scissors. Wrapped the girl in a towel she had taken from a house full of corpses. The baby girl looked at her with such large eyes and wonderment that Amy cried. She was beautiful and fragile, precious and frail.

The infected thing slammed against the walls. The doors rattled.

Exhausted, her heart swollen and her body trembling, Amy cradled the girl with one arm while she picked up the pistol. It was shaking in her hand. A door hinge snapped. A gaping mouth appeared through a torn hole then drew back.

Amy told her daughter that she loved her. Kissed her forehead and smelled the wonderful scent of her scalp.

"Welcome to the world," she said, holding back the hysteria behind her eyes.

Wood broke under the violence of blackened claws.

Amy had forgotten how many bullets were in the pistol. Whatever was left, it would have to be enough. If she had to, she would use the gun to club the infected to death. Nothing would take her baby away.

Her daughter looked up at her with the smallest curve of a smile.

Amy smiled in return. "Everything's going to be okay. I'll take care of you." Her voice wavered on the last word and she began to cry.

She aimed the pistol at the doors and waited, her vision wet with tears.

The sharp crack of splintering wood.

The doors flew open.

An infected man, alone and hungry, snarling through a slack mouth. Stink of decay and dirt. Deathly thin underneath the slashed and filthy remains of a funeral suit.

Amy kept her arm steady. The feel of the pistol in her hand. Looking down the barrel at the monster.

She remembered those who had died on the road.

The monster lurched forward.

The baby cried.

Amy pulled the trigger and said her daughter's name.

THE END

Acknowledgements

Many thanks to everyone who's ever supported my writing and bought my books. I'm immensely grateful to my friends and family for all the encouragement and help over the last few years. And lastly, cheers to my literary heroes, who continue to inspire me with their work.

You're all great people.

THE LAST OUTPOST

Rich Hawkins

Lightning Source UK Ltd.
Milton Keynes UK
UKOW02f0208060916

282310UK00005B/149/P